IN A RAKE'S EMBRACE

SINS & SENSIBILITIES
BOOK III

STACY REID

For my brother Ronald: I love you. We are more alike than we are different.

CHAPTER 1

Miss Agatha Woodville froze mid-step as she hurried from the room, her mind racing with thoughts of how to protect her younger sisters and their modest household. Their father's gambling debts had already cost them much, but when he staggered home last night with the news that he had lost everything, their fragile world collapsed. The dread in her father's eyes had stolen Agatha's sleep, and now, as morning light filtered through the drapes, she was bleary-eyed and desperate for a few hours of rest.

Her stepmother, Gloria, had come to Agatha a few minutes ago, saying a man had come to collect the debt. She had been tasked with discreetly eavesdropping on the conversation between him and her father. Agatha pressed her ear against the wooden door, straining to catch every word.

"I have three daughters," her father said, his voice weak with shame. "They are all lovely girls ..."

"Oh?" the man drawled. "How does this supposed loveliness cover the eighty pounds you owe, Mr. Wright?"

Eighty pounds was a fortune! How could her father dare to gamble with such a sum?

"Was it so much?"

The low chuckle from the other man was derisive. "That is only the principal."

"One of my daughters ..."

"One of your daughters what?"

Her father hesitated, his voice dropping to a mutter. "Everyone knows Mr. Wright is part owner of *Aphrodite*. My daughter, Maggie, can ... work the debt off there."

Agatha's heart squeezed. *Maggie?* Her sweet, innocent sixteen-year-old sister spent most days with her nose buried in a book she had read dozens of times. Maggie dreamed of becoming a premier modiste, designing gowns for actresses on the grand stages of the theatre. Not working in London. What was her father on about?

"Come now," the man replied smoothly, "we both know there's only one kind of work your daughter could do at *Aphrodite* to clear that debt in a year. Are you truly willing to send her there to earn it ... on her back?"

Agatha's breath caught. *On her back?* Her breath hitched, panic welling up inside her. She pushed her trembling hand against her mouth, stifling a gasp. It couldn't be. Her father wouldn't do that. Not to Maggie. Not to any of his children. Perhaps she had misunderstood, and the whispers she often overheard in the tavern didn't carry the same meaning as this man's words.

"If that's what needs to be done," her father said, his voice thin with defeat, "then it must be done."

Agatha could no longer stay hidden. Fury burned inside her chest, and she burst through the door before she could think better of it. Both men looked up, startled by her sudden appearance. The stranger's eyes widened when they landed on her, his lips curling into a smile. Though dressed respectably, something in his gaze made Agatha uneasy. He seemed cold and calculating.

"By God," he breathed, his gaze raking over her as if she were a prize on display. "She's *stunning*. You've been hiding a gold mine, Woodville, you *fool*."

Ignoring the man, Agatha directed her attention to her father. "What kind of work are you proposing for Maggie?" Her father's face reddened, and his gaze slid to the floor.

"Look at me, Papa!" Agatha demanded, her voice quivering. "What do you mean she would need to earn it on her back?"

He remained silent, unable to meet her regard. A terrible, choking pressure formed in her chest. "How can you even consider this? Maggie has only turned sixteen this month. How could you think of sending her away to cover your failings?"

The stranger interjected with a sly smile. "Is Maggie as lovely as this one? Because if not, she won't do."

"Do?" Agatha turned on him, anger blazing in her heart. "You will speak plainly what you want my sister to do!"

The man's smirk remained. "To work in one of Mr. Wright's pleasure palaces, of course. Until the debt is cleared."

Agatha's stomach lurched. *A pleasure palace.* She recalled the sly propositions directed her way and the coarse laughter of men sharing secrets they assumed no one else could hear. A woman earning a living on her back was hardly a euphemism for anything honorable. "Do you mean ... a *brothel?*"

His silence spoke volumes. She stumbled back and collapsed onto the threadbare sofa behind her, the cushions beneath her feeling more unforgiving than ever. The room seemed to spin as she tried to catch her breath.

"This is madness," she whispered. "I will not send my sister to do something so vile and beneath her dignity. How do you even think it, Papa? *How?*"

The man's eyes gleamed. "Then perhaps you'll go in her place. Mr. Wright's debts must be paid, one way or another."

"No!" her father shouted, his voice cracking with despair. "Not Aga! She's to be married. A respectable young man has asked for her hand ..."

Agatha curled her hands into tight fists. Her engagement had been little more than an arrangement of convenience. Mr. David Trenton was a schoolmaster in their village and had been sweet to her for the last few months. She had taken a few walks with him and had even attended a country dance in the public rooms of the village square, where he had danced with her three times. That was enough to send everyone in their small town to start talking about a wedding and their future children.

Agatha found David good-natured and pleasant but felt no rousing emotions or excitement whenever she thought of spending the rest of her life with him. Her stepmother had counseled that they needed more help and that love would grow. Trusting in those reassurances, Agatha informed him she would marry him.

"Is that true?" the man asked, staring at her.

Her father rushed forward. "My daughter here is the eldest, and she will soon have a respectable marriage. She cannot go in ... in her younger sister's place. I will only approve of Maggie leaving."

Her father's desperation cut through her.

"How can you be so cold-hearted," she whispered, more to herself than anyone else. "So ruthless to your child?"

Her father's head snapped up at her words, his eyes gleaming with tears. "I can't lose you, Aga."

Her chest constricted with hurt. "But you can lose Maggie?" she snapped, her voice cracking. "Maggie is *not* leaving. I will not allow it, Papa."

His gaze narrowed, and his nostrils flared. "Margaret is my daughter and, by right of law, my property; I make whatever decision necessary to save this family!"

Agatha's heart ached. The truth was in the silence that followed, like a knife twisting inside her. She was no stranger to broken promises or unfulfilled dreams. It had always been painfully clear that her father held little affection for his daughters. One might have assumed that Carson, his only son, would have been his pride and joy, yet even Carson received indifference. Their father made no plans for his future and left his education entirely in her hands.

Agatha had always known that Maggie—who bore fewer of their mother's features than she or Sarah—was treated with even less warmth. But to send Maggie to a place like that ...

Agatha would never forgive her father.

The man, growing impatient, leaned forward. "Either Agatha or Maggie will leave with me. Someone will be leaving this house today."

Her father flinched. "Not Aga!"

Tears welled in Agatha's eyes. It had come to this. Her father was willing to sacrifice her sister —his daughter—for his own mistakes. The weight of it was crushing. Agatha had savings, laboriously acquired from the perfumed sachets she sold. She had to prepare for her siblings' future, as her father seemed determined to squander it away. It would pain her to start over or lose any of it, but she was willing to do anything to save her sister.

"I have some money saved," she said quietly. "It is not the full amount, but—"

"No."

Agatha had sixty pounds, and it had taken her three years of diligence to set that money aside. She hoped to offer it and suggest a bargain where she could work that remainder off. She stood on shaky legs, squaring her shoulders, and turned to face the man. "Please, sir, we—"

"My employer gave me a task," the man said with icy disdain. "Return with the money in full ... or his body."

Agatha's breath hitched, and she recoiled as the man's sharp gaze cut into her.

"Consider this," he added, his tone unsettlingly calm, "with your beauty, you could earn the sum in a single night. It might take your sister months."

A sharp tremor ran through her body. The thought—horrifying and vile—crept into her mind before she could stop it.

Perhaps it might be better if Mr. Wright did whatever he wanted with him!

She squeezed her eyes shut, disgusted with herself. No matter how despicable her father had become, no matter the shame he'd brought upon their family with his gambling and lies, he was still their father. The children needed him, especially in a society that left women vulnerable without the protection of a man. Agatha knew this all too well—Mr. Randall, the owner of their humble cottage, had refused to rent it to her directly. Only when he spoke to her father had Mr. Randall reluctantly agreed.

A woman alone couldn't even secure a roof over her head. How absurd. And yet, it was true. Despite his failings, her father's presence was crucial to their survival. Without him, they would be lost.

A breath-crushing tension wrapped its cruel arms around her. "I will go with you," Agatha said quietly, her voice barely above a whisper. "To repay the debt."

"No!" her father shouted, his voice panicked as he rushed toward her.

His hand clamped down on her shoulder, shaking her roughly. "You don't understand, Agatha! You can't—"

Wrenching free from his grip, Agatha glared at him, her anger spiking. "You do not get to decide for me! You do not get to sacrifice Maggie for your disgusting habit. You should be ashamed to face your children. Mama would be—"

The slap came out of nowhere, sharp and sudden, snapping her head to the side. Silence filled the room as her father stumbled back, his eyes wide with horror at what he'd done. He collapsed onto the worn sofa, his body shaking with sobs.

The man looked on, unmoved. "You have an

hour," he said, his voice like steel. "I'll await you in my carriage outside."

Agatha didn't acknowledge him. Instead, she walked out of the parlor and into the small kitchen, where her stepmother, Gloria, and her siblings sat around the breakfast table. Sarah, twelve years old, was cheerfully spooning the last of her porridge into her mouth while Carson, only five, sat beside her, swinging his legs beneath the chair.

"Sarah," Agatha said, her voice steady, "take Carson to the garden to play."

Sarah's eyes lit up, and without question, she finished her porridge in a hurry, grabbed Carson's hand, and darted out the back door. Agatha watched them leave, her heart aching, knowing their innocence wouldn't last forever. She couldn't bear for them to know their father's cruelty yet, not until they were much older.

"What is it, Agatha?" Gloria asked, her voice tight with worry as she gripped her hands in her lap.

Agatha hesitated for a moment, then quickly explained the situation. Maggie, sitting across the table, went pale. She leaped to her feet and rushed over, clutching Agatha's hands.

"You can't go, Aga. You can't!"

Agatha gently tucked a stray wisp of dark blonde hair behind her younger sister's ear, offering a soft smile. Agatha had the resilience to suppress the torment that gnawed at the depths of her heart and must never show her family how terrified she was.

"I'm going, Maggie. I told you because I need you and Gloria to be careful. Don't trust Papa anymore. He's not thinking clearly."

"But you're supposed to be married," Maggie whispered, her voice trembling. "What will David think? What if he finds out? I should go instead."

"No," Agatha said firmly. "You will do no such thing. I'm your older sister. It's my job to protect you." She cupped Maggie's face in her hands, her heart breaking at the sight of her sister's tear-filled eyes. "I love you more than anything, Maggie. And I promise this won't be a hardship for me."

Her sister's lips trembled. "Do you know what to do?"

"I am older than you."

"That is not an answer, Aga."

She gently tapped her sister's chin. "I know enough."

Maggie threw herself into Agatha's arms, her small frame shaking with sobs. Agatha held her tightly, stroking her hair, meeting Gloria's gaze across the room. The sorrow and pity she saw in her stepmother's eyes nearly undid her. She had to be strong. For Maggie. For Sarah and Carson. For all of them.

Once Maggie calmed, Agatha sent her to join the others outside. Gloria handed her a bowl of porridge, and they sat silently at the small wooden table. Agatha ate quickly, her mind already preparing for what was to come.

"Is it terrible?" Agatha asked softly after a long pause, her voice barely audible. "Being with a man?"

Gloria looked at her, her expression thoughtful. "No, it's not terrible. It can be ... pleasant. But the first time—it might hurt."

Agatha nodded, swallowing the lump in her throat. "Badly?"

"You will forget it by the next day."

"I see." She cleared her throat. "Is it ... is it quick?"

"It can be. It depends on the man."

Silence fell, and several beats passed before her stepmother cleared her throat.

"Aga," Gloria said softly. "You must never tell David about what happens in London. As a man, they have this notion that we women are to be pure when they are allowed to sow their seeds."

Agatha's belly knotted. "I will tell him the truth. I will not blame him if he wishes not to marry me after."

"There are ways to fake your chastity," Gloria said insistently. "A vial of chicken blood with a few strategic drops will do the trick. There is no need to tell him anything when the entirety of Cringleford knows Mrs. Murphey is currently his lover. Who is he to demand that you remain pure for him when he still takes up with that woman though he is affianced?"

Agatha nodded, understanding her stepmother's advice. Even so, until she spoke with David, she couldn't be certain of her choice. She couldn't dwell on the enormity of what she was about to do. Not now. She finished her meal and stood, heading to the small bedroom she shared with her sisters. She dressed in her best gown—a simple blue muslin—and slipped on her worn boots, the soles nearly gone from overuse. Her cloak, too tight around the shoulders, was the only one she had. She tugged it on, ignoring how it pinched at the seams.

Stepping outside, Agatha glanced at the carriage waiting, its wheels caked in mud from the village roads. The man stood beside it, his eyes following her every movement, but she refused to meet his gaze. Her heart hammered in her chest as she crossed the yard, the weight of her decision pressing down on her with each step. This was the only way.

As she approached the carriage, determination filled her. Whatever awaited her in London, she would endure it for her family. It had been her promise, after all, when her mother had died days after giving birth to Sarah. Agatha, just nine years old at the time, had held her mother's hand as she lay on her deathbed, vowing through her tears that she would care for and love her sisters always.

That promise had never left her, and it never would.

CHAPTER 2

The journey from the small seaside town of Cringleford to London lasted several hours, the carriage bumping along the uneven roads. The man beside her had attempted to engage her in conversation, but Agatha kept her eyes firmly on the passing scenery, her face an indifferent mask as she stared out the window.

Now, she sat in the grand drawing room on the second floor of *Aphrodite*, a pleasure palace. The sheer opulence of the place was beyond anything her imagination had conjured. She had expected something gaudy and tasteless, but the reality was far more stunning—and unsettling. The four-story building radiated decadence. From the moment she stepped inside, her breath had been snatched away. The walls were draped with sumptuous tapestries, the ceilings painted with scenes depicting conquests and wild revelry.

The atmosphere hummed with life, unlike any country dance she had ever attended. On the ground floor, men in the finest fashion mingled with women dressed in exquisite gowns, their hair styled into elaborate coifs. The candlelight from the grand chandeliers above cast a golden glow over their forms. Couples danced to an orchestra's tune, but there was something different—scandalous—about how the women leaned into their partners, how closely they moved together.

It had an air of elegance but felt undeniably … forbidden.

Now, she waited in a smaller drawing room on the second floor, which, while still elegant, was furnished more simply. Velvet chairs and a fainting couch sat beneath a large, gilded mirror, reflecting the firelight that danced in the hearth. She fidgeted slightly; her hands clenched in her lap as dread pooled in her chest.

The door opened, and a woman entered with a confident sway. She appeared to be around forty years old, her face touched only lightly by time, with a few delicate lines around her eyes. Her dark blonde hair was piled high in an intricate style, adorned with jewels, and her gown—deep burgundy and scandalously low-cut

—clung to her voluptuous frame, barely covering her ample bosom.

"By God, Albert, you were right. She's a prize," the woman said, her voice smooth as silk.

Her sharp gaze swept over Agatha as if she were appraising livestock.

Agatha stood and lifted her chin, determined not to show her fear. "I am Miss Woodville. Are you the person in charge here?"

The woman's lips curled into a slow smile, her eyes gleaming with amusement. "I am Madam Rebecca," she said, her voice dripping with authority. "Smile, let me see your teeth."

Agatha complied reluctantly, her jaw tight.

"Very good," Madam Rebecca said, nodding approvingly. "Do you understand what is required of you?"

Agatha's stomach clenched, but she refused to falter. "No."

"You're in *Aphrodite*, a pleasure palace," the madam said, her tone businesslike and condescending. "We cater to the refined tastes of high-society gentlemen. Whatever desires they have can be fulfilled within these walls."

"So ... a brothel," Agatha replied tightly, the word tasting like ash on her tongue.

"A brothel?" Madam Rebecca scoffed, raising an imperious brow. "That suggests a common house for lowborn women. I assure you, I am anything but common."

Agatha had no reply. The sickening dread coiled tighter around her chest. This was the place her father had intended to send her sister.

"Your father owes my business partner a significant sum that must be paid tonight," the madam continued, her voice cold and clipped. "I tried to negotiate an extension after I learned Mr. Woodville sent his daughter to repay the debt, but Mr. Wright refuses to delay further. It has already been extended three times, and his compassion will set a bad precedent. Do you understand what that means?"

Agatha's throat tightened. "No. I have some money ... Could I speak to Mr. Wright to propose another arrangement? One that ... doesn't involve me selling myself?"

The words felt scraped from somewhere deep inside her.

Madam Rebecca's eyes narrowed slightly. "Oh? And how much money do you have?"

"I have sixty pounds," Agatha said, desperation creeping into her voice, "and I can—"

"Two hundred pounds," the madam interrupted.

The room seemed to tilt, and Agatha gripped the arm of the chair to steady herself.

"*Two hundred pounds?* But the man who came to our home said the debt was eighty pounds."

Madam Rebecca's expression didn't waver. "Interest," she said. "One hundred and twenty pounds in interest."

Agatha's blood boiled with helpless fury. "Your business partner is a thief! How can the debt have more than doubled in such a short time?"

"I have nothing to do with the terms of the loan," the madam said coolly. "That's Mr. Wright's concern. But I assure you, the full amount must be paid tonight, or your father will not live to see morning."

Agatha felt as though the walls were closing in around her.

"Many of the ladies here prove their worth quickly," Madam Rebecca added. "Please the right man and one might even take you as his mistress. It's what many aim for. A life of comfort."

"No," Agatha whispered.

The madam's eyes flashed with impatience. "Then Mr. Wright will be free to handle your father however he sees fit."

Would the gambling den owner truly have her father killed? Surely ... surely, such a world of ruthlessness did not exist?

"One night," Agatha gasped, recalling the

man's words from earlier. "He said I could earn it in one night. He said, given my beauty, it was possible."

Madam Rebecca considered her for a long moment before responding. "Wait here. I'll see what can be done."

Agatha sank back into the chaise, her fingers gripping the fabric so tightly that her knuckles turned white. She fought to keep the panic at bay, closing her eyes and picturing the seaside from her childhood—the sound of the waves, the feel of the cool breeze—anything to take her mind away from this nightmare.

The door creaked open, and she stood quickly.

"You're in luck," Madam Rebecca said with a slight smile. "One of our more discerning and distinguished clients is here tonight. He's tired and seeking something new. If you please him, you'll see only him this evening."

Relief flooded Agatha's chest. One man. It was still abhorrent but far easier to endure than being passed from one to another.

The madam handed her a simple white gown made of fine silk that felt rich against her skin. Thankfully, it wasn't overly revealing. Agatha quickly removed her worn boots and clothes, folding them neatly to the side. Madam Rebecca gathered them up and tossed them out the door without saying what she did with her clothes.

"Come with me," the madam instructed.

Agatha took a deep breath, squared her shoulders, and followed. She had no choice now but to step forward into this terrifying world, her heart heavy with hopelessness.

One year later ...

AGATHA SAT at the worn kitchen table, her head bowed as she stared at the small ledger. The numbers swam before her eyes, and a tight knot of worry coiled in her stomach. The money she had carefully budgeted over the past year was dwindling, and with the unexpected rent increase, the future looked bleak.

"How bad is it?" Gloria asked from across the table, her voice quiet but filled with concern. "I have never seen you look so down, Aga."

She took a deep breath and rubbed a hand over her tired eyes before responding. "With the rent increase ... we'll only have a few coins left for food to last for a month, perhaps six weeks if we practice strict economy. There is not enough for firewood or new bedding for the winter. Sarah also needs new boots."

The summer was already cold in the nights, and she could not imagine how they would fear for the upcoming winter.

"The larder is almost empty. We can buy a sack of potatoes, flour, and rice. Mrs. Pottinger says we can take more oranges and apples from her grove. There are not enough coins for meat, and we cannot risk taking quail from the squire's land again. The risk of being charged for poaching is too great."

Gloria sighed, her hands resting in her lap as she stared at the empty fireplace. "That's ... not good, is it?"

"No," Agatha said, her voice barely above a whisper. Her heart kicked painfully against her ribs.

It is terrifying.

A sudden shriek of laughter broke the tense silence. Agatha glanced out the small window, her gaze softening as she watched her younger siblings playing outside. Sarah and Maggie were running through the field, chasing after a kite, with little Carson trailing behind them, his face glowing with joy.

A small smile tugged at her lips. Despite their laughter, the weight of responsibility pressed heavily on her shoulders.

They're happy now, but how long can I keep this up?

The past year had been a difficult one. They had arrived in Devonshire with little more than hope due to the monies she had saved. Agatha had worked tirelessly to provide for her siblings. She had taken up sewing work as she had done back in their small seaside town, repairing and making garments for the local villagers. Gloria and Maggie helped, too, but it was never enough with six mouths to feed and rent to pay. Carson suffered a recent bout of illness, and the physician's fee had been exorbitant.

Agatha had been careful, budgeting every penny, ensuring they had enough to survive. But with winter approaching, their situation was becoming more precarious. They had moved to a small cottage on the outskirts of the village, nestled against the moors. It was humble, but it had been their sanctuary for the past year. The idea of losing it, of being forced to uproot her family once again, filled her with dread.

Gloria reached across the table, gently covering Agatha's hand with hers. "We'll manage, somehow. We always do."

Agatha nodded, though doubt gnawed at her. She had vowed to protect her siblings; to keep them safe from the horrors their father had nearly subjected them to, but now she wasn't sure if she could continue to provide for them. While her sewing and perfumed sachets brought in some income, it was never enough to cover the growing costs.

I can't fail them. I won't.

Her thoughts drifted to the night she was taken to *Aphrodite*. The gentleman Madam Rebecca had taken her to that fateful night was a duke. Agatha only learned of his identity when the coachman, at his command, escorted her back home. The duke had paid the madam in full, settling the debt her father owed, but in a surprising twist, he'd informed Agatha that he did not need her services.

Relief had washed over her so powerfully that tears had slipped down her cheeks. She had expected the worst that night, steeling herself for what she thought would be a soul-crushing experience, only to find unexpected kindness in a man who owed her nothing. The tears of relief had continued to fall during the long journey back home. She hadn't seen the duke since that night and did not expect ever to encounter him again. Sometimes, when she lay awake at night, she thought of him. Why had he helped her leave? Why had he paid her father's debt and sent her away without asking for anything in return? Why had he given her banknotes?

She didn't even know his name. But she owed him more than she could ever repay.

It had been a night of immense relief and the beginning of her new life. She had expected her father to be at home, wallowing in shame over what he had forced his daughter to endure. But instead, he had been snarling and angry. The following morning, he had left, returning to the gambling halls of London, where he would often disappear for weeks at a time. Her father had also pilfered the banknotes the duke had given her. Agatha had sobbed until her throat felt raw. Thankfully, he had not discovered the other monies she saved.

Disgust, horror, and betrayal had settled in her chest, heavier than the relief she had felt. Her father hadn't learned his lesson. The danger was far from over. That morning, as she looked at her younger siblings, blissfully unaware of what had almost happened, Agatha realized she couldn't allow them to remain under his control. If their father could easily offer Maggie to settle his debts, what would stop him from repeating the same?

Agatha had taken control, determined to forge a better future for herself and her siblings. The decision had been made swiftly. They had packed their few belongings—just enough to fit into a small cart and escaped. Agatha left her father a note explaining that she had taken her siblings away for their safety. She wrote only so he wouldn't worry—though she doubted he would care enough to feel concerned.

She didn't tell him where they were going. He didn't deserve to know. With quiet resolve, she led her family far from the small seaside town they had known, all the way to Devonshire, where no one knew their names and no debts or danger loomed over them.

Gloria had brought her younger brother Henry to live with them out of fear for his well-being under the care of their eldest brother, a butcher. At just fourteen years old, Henry had been working grueling twelve-hour days for only a few shillings a month. Over time, Agatha came to love him as if he were her brother. His presence alone, often seen from a distance, discouraged trouble from finding them. Even their landlord seemed to believe it was Henry with whom he had the rental agreement.

But as the months passed, the struggle to survive became more difficult. She had always known it wouldn't be easy, but the weight of that knowledge felt heavier with each passing day.

"What are you thinking about?" Gloria asked gently.

"That night in London and the duke who helped me," Agatha said with a self-deprecating smile. "He said something to me, and I did not believe him, but it has proven true."

When he had offered her money, her fierce pride had pushed her to ask for a job instead.

"*Too beautiful,*" he had snapped. "*You would toss my household into disorder and have my footmen turn into competing fools.*"

"*I see. Perhaps a recommendation to be a governess—*"

"*The master of the home you work in will have you on your back within days. Unless you choose to hide your figure as best possible, disfigure your face, or find a kind widow who has no preying sons.*"

"*I would never consent to an affair!*"

"*He would not care if you were willing. You have no power or connection.*"

Gloria shifted restlessly. "What did he say?"

"The duke warned me how difficult it would be to work for others," Agatha said softly, shaking her head. "He made it seem like my beauty was a *curse*. He said if I worked in anyone's household, I'd cause an uproar. I was a housekeeper for Squire Portman for just a week, and he was determined to make me his lover despite his wife being heavy with child. And look at what happened at the baker's shop— three workers, men I gave no attention to, fought over me. It's nonsensical. It's as if they've decided I have no say in the matter. Mrs.

Bramley ordered several gowns from you, but when I delivered them, she was so furious that her husband ogled me that she refused to pay. It is most *absurd,* but it is very much real."

Gloria frowned deeply. "Why are you thinking about this now?"

Agatha hesitated, her gaze drifting down to the ledger, showing the harsh reality of their future. "The duke ... said my beauty is power if I knew how to use it."

Her stepmother inhaled sharply, her eyes widening in surprise. "What?"

"Beauty is a power. A man would willingly pay two hundred pounds to spend a night with you," the duke had told her. *"Entice and allure. Craft a reputation as a woman who is both unattainable and unavailable. Tease and tempt, and let men be willing to pay just to behold your beauty ... to hear you play the pianoforte. Declare to the world that you are a virgin, and they will clamor at your door for the mere chance to be the one to seduce you."*

Taking a steadying breath, Agatha met Gloria's gaze. "I'm going to London."

Her stepmother stiffened, her lips parting as if to protest, but no objection came.

"Wait for my letters," Agatha continued, her voice firm yet gentle. "I will send them frequently, along with money."

"What will you do?"

"I should not tell you about it," she said gently. "I will not do anything dangerous."

"How can you be so certain you'll make any money? This is too risky and reckless—"

"Am I beautiful, Gloria?"

Gloria blinked, then nodded slowly. "I have never seen anyone to equal you."

Agatha swallowed tightly. "Do ... do men covet beautiful things?"

"Yes," Gloria whispered, her voice thick with emotion.

"I've had a year to realize what I've been doing isn't enough. We have no connections, no one to turn to. We can only rely on ourselves. I can only rely on what I have." Agatha's voice grew stronger, more resolved. "Fortunately, my mother spent countless hours educating me so I could read, do arithmetic and even speak French. I know there is much more I need to learn. And I must go to London. We'll tell the girls I'm going for a respectable position in town, and everything will be fine."

Tears glistened in Gloria's eyes, and she reached out to clasp Agatha's hand. "I'll take care of everyone, Aga. You won't have to worry about a thing."

"I know," Agatha said softly, squeezing her hand in return. "I know."

Gloria never hesitated to leave their father

behind. She had taken on much of the housework and cooking, filling the role their family needed. Together, they shared a silent understanding. Agatha would take this risk, not for herself but for all of them.

CHAPTER 3

Thomas Pennington, the Earl of Radbourne, stilled, the glass of brandy he had been refilling, momentarily forgotten. The liquid splashed onto the polished walnut table, and he set the decanter down with an irritated hiss. Reclining against the sofa, he regarded Madam Rebecca with curiosity and disbelief scything through him. It was as though she were some strange, unfamiliar creature.

"You want me to teach a lady the art of seduction ... without seducing her?" he repeated, his tone dry. "What nonsense is this?"

Madam Rebecca crossed her legs at the knee and smiled serenely. "I thought you were the best person to help with her needs."

He arched a brow. "Is that so?"

"Absolutely," she replied, taking a delicate sip of her champagne. "You're a rake through and

31

through, with a fondness for women in all their forms. But unlike most, you aren't led solely by your cock. You can be discerning, and you have restraint. This lady will be auctioning her virginity and ... expertise in six weeks."

Thomas chuckled, his interest mildly piqued. "A virgin with expertise? Now, that is something I've never heard of. Or perhaps I have. Two of your ladies boasted the same a few months ago. Wasn't there a fight in the card rooms about who truly took Lady Hettie's chastity?"

"I daresay, it's little scuffles like that which convince me this auction will be brilliant—and talked about for months." Madam Rebecca cleared her throat lightly. "Miss Woodville is a beauty, and she's educated—but not enough to hold her own in a conversation with the fine gentlemen of the *ton*. She'll walk among them on the floors, and they will want her, knowing the auction is imminent. She will be the prize."

"So, you want me to teach her the art of what? Flirtation? Seduction?"

"Yes ... without touching her," she replied with a pointed look.

Thomas smiled, amusement rushing through him. "There will be touching. It would be impossible otherwise."

"Must you touch her?"

"Of course, when have I ever said I was some selfless gent?"

"Yes, but you must not ravish her," she warned.

He smiled slightly. "I am suitably bored to be intrigued. What's in it for me?"

"Relieving your boredom, of course," she said sweetly, her brown eyes gleaming with calculation. "Do you think I have not noticed? You visit our halls less since Lord Ambrose and His Grace Basil married. You visit the card rooms and gamble but have not taken a woman in almost three months."

"How interesting that you keep a record of my cockstands. Have you never thought I might be finding my pleasure elsewhere?"

"No." She waved a hand. "There is no reason to stare at me with such coldness, Radbourne. My business is knowing when I am on the cusp of losing most valued client. I want to keep you happy, my lord. I have already lost Basil and Ambrose. I think you will be suitably ... challenged with tutoring Miss Woodville. There will be some pleasure for you because she will need to practice some things. I trust that you would never ravish her."

It was mildly interesting Madam Rebecca knew some of his character. "And what is in this for you?"

33

"Fifty percent of whatever Miss Woodville earns from the highest bidder. I'll provide her with private quarters on the fourth floor, setting her apart from the other ladies. That she will have her boudoir on my floor will be the first signal that she is different. She'll have a handsome apartment with a bedchamber, sitting room, and music room. Meals will be provided whenever she wants, and a burly footman will be assigned to protect her from unwanted advances. Twice a month, we host musicales or our version of it. Her debut will be a performance to whet their appetites—she'll sing and dance. She has a lovely voice, though I was surprised to learn she doesn't play any instrument, as many young ladies do. She suggested learning to dance to add something unique to her performance."

"The waltz?" he asked, lifting a brow. "Never say I am to be her partner in this."

Her mouth quirked. "That, and another— one that will shock and entice."

"What sort of dance?" Thomas asked, skeptical. He'd never been one to believe that dancing could hold much power beyond a tiresome prelude to courtship.

"A dance that requires someone to play the flute," she replied, her lips curling into another knowing smile.

"Of course. And you know I play the flute," he said drily.

"Yes," she said, her smile deepening.

"Is this your plan?" he asked, narrowing his eyes.

"Miss Woodville approached me," Rebecca replied, a bemused look entering her expression. "We met under ... less-than-ideal circumstances last year, and I was surprised to see her again. She laid out her business proposal, and I listened. I'm a woman of vision, and she is determined. I believe she can succeed."

"You still haven't told me what dance she's learning that can entice men more than the waltz."

Madam Rebecca's eyes gleamed mischievously. "An eastern dance I learned some years ago."

Thomas arched a brow. There had been a long-standing rumor that Rebecca had spent five years in the harem of a pasha, learning sensual dances involving sinuous movements of the hips and belly. Most believed it was merely a story to enhance her allure—no one had ever seen this dance.

"I'll need to see her," Thomas said, curiosity now fully piqued.

Rebecca gave a nod, rose gracefully from her

chair, and opened the door. It seemed Miss Woodville had been waiting just outside.

"Agatha, please come in and meet Lord Radbourne."

The young lady entered, and for a moment, it felt like the air had been snatched from Thomas's lungs. An unexpected pulse of heat settled on the base of his cock, and he ruthlessly pushed aside the sensation. He slowly rose to his feet, his eyes never leaving her. She met his gaze, her chin lifting defiantly, but he didn't miss the wild flutter of her pulse at her slender throat. Despite her attempt at poise, there was an unmistakable tension in her stance— nervousness she was trying to conceal. He studied her closely, noting her attempt to project confidence and the vulnerability in her eyes.

She lowered into a curtsy. "Lord Radbourne. A delight to make your acquaintance."

Her accent wasn't refined, betraying her unfamiliarity with the polished circles of the *ton*, and even in the way she held herself, there was a sense of someone unaccustomed to the world she was about to enter. It struck him that she was like a lamb surrounded by wolves, unaware of the dangers that lurked, waiting to devour her.

What madness has driven her to do this?

The thought came unbidden, but he pushed it away swiftly. He didn't allow himself to get involved with women anymore—not beyond the mutual satisfaction they shared. Emotional entanglements were a complication Thomas no longer tolerated; in his mind, curiosity was the gateway to such entanglements. He had no intention of delving beneath the surface.

If he accepted this, it would remain purely transactional. Nothing more. Or perhaps it simply flattered his vanity and self-conceit to tutor such a ravishing beauty. "I will meet with Miss Woodville alone."

"Of course," Rebecca replied with a knowing smile, dipping her head before leaving them. The door closed softly behind her.

Silence settled between them as they took each other's measure. She was dressed in a light blue, diaphanous silk gown that flowed over her form, modest in its coverage yet undeniably seductive. The neckline dipped just enough to reveal the delicate curve of her throat and a tantalizing hint of cleavage. Her bare toes curled into the rich carpet, a small, telling gesture of discomfort.

By God, she was one of the most stunning women he had ever seen. And he had seen plenty. Her beauty wasn't just in her flawless features but in the dichotomy between her boldness and the vulnerability she couldn't fully hide. Her green eyes—wide with defiance and uncertainty, held his.

"Take down your hair," he commanded softly, his voice betraying none of the effect her presence had on him.

Her eyes slightly narrowed, but she obeyed, lifting her hands to remove the few pins holding her hair in place. The heavy tresses tumbled free, cascading over her shoulders in dark, silken waves that spilled down her back, reaching her waist. The sight only heightened her allure, making her look untamed and impossibly more beautiful. Her skin was delicate and creamy pale, her lips lush and sweetly curved, and her slender figure graced with just the right amount of fullness in all the places that would make a man pause. That gaze was apprehensive and impossibly innocent—this woman did not belong here.

"You're truly a virgin," he stated, his tone flat though his pulse quickened.

Somehow, he had thought it a ruse, the allure she would use to tempt clients. Many ladies at *Aphrodite* pretended to be many things they were not, and the illusions often made their clients happy. Thomas knew of five different men who all claimed to deflower Lady Hettie.

He arched a brow. "Do you speak?"

Miss Woodville's cheeks flushed, a soft pink rising on her face as her green eyes glittered beneath her lashes like emerald flames. "Yes."

"You are the one who asked for someone to teach you?"

"Yes," she replied, her voice steady despite the deepening flush on her skin.

"This entire business arrangement with Madam Rebecca was your idea?"

"Yes."

He raked his fingers through his hair, expelling a sharp breath. "If you are being forced, now is the best time to tell me when we are alone. I will help—"

"No one is forcing me. I approached Madam Rebecca, my lord."

Thomas walked to the mantel and poured himself a glass of whisky. He lifted the glass toward her. "Would you care for a drink?"

Miss Woodville winced, and she shook her head. "No, thank you, my lord. I do not drink."

He took a healthy swallow of his whisky. "Madam Rebecca has a wealth of carnal knowledge. Why are you not relying on her expertise?"

The idea of teaching her himself was dangerous—too dangerous. Being so close to her, demonstrating how to kiss, how to arouse desire in a man, all while denying his own instincts, would be nothing short of torture. He understood his sexual limits, and this woman could push him well beyond them. *It is bloody laughable*. How could he be so certain when they had never touched? And that irritated Thomas.

"Staring at me does not provide an answer, Miss Woodville."

She delicately cleared her throat. "Madam Rebecca is not from the *ton*. And neither am I, my lord. She explained all her clients here are men from high society. There is no lady from your society I could approach for lessons in such things."

"What things are those?"

She tucked a wisp of hair behind her ear. "I … how to speak better, walk gracefully, and clothe myself with elegance. Madam Rebecca explained that her clients seek women who seem … refined and exceptional. Women who speak and carry themselves like those in the *ton* but with a hint of allure far more provocative than ladies of quality. They don't come here solely for … carnal indulgences. They come for the music, the conversation, and the company that feels both elevated and enticingly unrestrained. So, a gentleman from the *ton* would be far more appropriate to help me. I merely asked Rebecca to recommend someone skilled and honorable who wouldn't exploit my inexperience. She believed you to be that man, sir."

Her words were a challenge, almost daring him to refuse, but there was also a quiet plea in her gaze—one that unsettled Thomas. She knew what she was asking, yet she had no real idea of the world she was stepping into or the dangers she would face. He felt a pang of something unexpected—concern. It was fleeting, but there. She was far too innocent for what she sought, yet her determination was undeniable.

What had driven her to such desperation?

The question lingered, but he shoved it aside. He wasn't here to understand her motives.

"Will you help me, my lord?" she asked softly.

"I am considering it."

Her toes curled deeper into the carpet. "Do you ... do you need payment? I am happy to share the monies—"

"Do not insult me."

Those lovely green eyes widened. "That was not my intention."

Thomas frowned into his drink, feeling the duality of wariness and interest stirring inside him. He was never indecisive—his decisions were typically pragmatic, logical and unapologetic. Yet now, he questioned himself. Why the hesitation? He could teach her but must maintain a careful distance emotionally and physically.

Thomas stilled as the realization struck. *Ah, there it is.*

His initial reaction to her had been an unbidden surge of hunger before he suppressed it. Thomas had always enjoyed women, enough so that his friends teased him about being a connoisseur of female beauty, a rake and debaucher. But despite his appreciation for pleasure, he never allowed himself to be consumed by it. Once, he had been foolish enough to believe he loved a woman—a belief shattered when she betrayed him and hurt someone he held dear. It had been a brutal lesson that led him to maintain a particular distance from women ever since, no matter how indulgent his pursuits.

But this woman ... this powerful attraction ... even the woman he thought he had loved hadn't stirred him so on a physical level. He slashed a glance toward Miss Woodville, and she instinctively stepped back, lifting a trembling hand to her throat. That small gesture made her seem delicate, more vulnerable even, and suddenly he felt like a damn beast. She didn't deserve his coldness. Her beauty wasn't her fault, nor was his reaction to it. A low sound of irritation escaped him as he downed the whisky in one long swallow, savoring the burn as it unraveled the cold knot of rage that always tightened within him when thoughts of Lady Eva and her betrayal resurfaced.

Thomas opened his mouth to dismiss Miss Woodville, but before he could speak, she rushed forward, her hand lifted in a silent plea as if sensing his intention.

"Please, sir ... *please*," she whispered, her voice strained, and her hands clenched at her sides.

He could almost smell the desperation on her, and his lips curled, hating how his heart wrenched at her distress. Thomas raked a hand through his hair. Could she truly understand what she was walking into? Or had her naïvety led her to deceive herself?

❧

AGATHA WISHED Madam Rebecca had better prepared her for the sheer presence of the Earl of Radbourne. He wasn't at all what she had expected—in truth, she hadn't even allowed herself to imagine him. To her, he had been a means to an end, a necessary guide on this path she had chosen. The earl seemed impeccably refined in his appearance, from the perfectly tailored jacket accentuating his broad shoulders and burgundy waistcoat to the gleaming polished boots. Yet beneath that elegance, there was something almost savagely carnal about him, a raw energy lurking behind his slanting cheekbones and sharp, direct stare. He was so large, masculine and beautiful.

His green eyes, cold and piercing, unsettled her. They seemed to strip her bare as though he could see straight through her, uncovering every secret and insecurity. Worse, that gaze stirred a sensation low in her belly, a flutter she didn't understand—one that unnerved her.

"*He is a handsome gentleman with reputed sexual prowess,*" Madam Rebecca had said. "*I know him to be a man of honor who is also ... very considerate of the fairer sex. That is crucial in the tutor who will help you. Do you agree, Miss Woodville?*"

"*Reputed? You are not certain he ... he ... is a good lover?*" Agatha had stammered, her blushes betraying her innocence.

The madam's smile had been knowing and amused. "*Sadly, I have never had the pleasure.*"

Their conversation had been brief and direct, leaving Agatha with little impression of the man before her. But now, standing in his presence, she was acutely aware of how disturbingly handsome he was. Even the jagged scar running from his brow down his cheek added to his allure, giving him an air of danger.

It didn't mar his beauty; it enhanced it, making him seem even more untouchable and, unfortunately, unapproachable.

"I want to understand what you want, Miss Woodville, so we have no misunderstanding. You want me to teach you how to seduce a lover? How to laugh and flirt with gentlemen. How to hide that you are not a lady of quality but could be whoever they wanted you to be in that moment."

His voice was low, edged with a hint of skepticism.

"Yes." Agatha swallowed, forcing herself to move a step closer. Her pulse raced, and she fought to steady her voice. "I want ... I want my lover to believe the nights spent with me were worth every penny he paid. Madam Rebecca cautioned me that while many men like the notion of taking a virgin to their bed, they do not want a lady to lay back stiffly and think of their duties. Apparently, this is a thing most men complain about their wives who ... were chaste. Rebecca agreed that the auction is a brilliant idea and will titillate many. However, I should balance my ... innocence with carnal skills. I agree wholeheartedly."

His lips quirked slightly as if amused by her boldness. "And how much money do you want, hmm?"

Agatha inhaled deeply and lifted her chin. "Five thousand pounds."

Lord Radbourne blinked, and then a slow, rich chuckle escaped him. He brought the glass of whisky to his lips, his gaze never leaving her. It was a long, insolent look—one that swept over her body as if appraising her like a possession. His stare was provoking, challenging, as though daring her to believe she could command such a sum.

For a moment, she felt exposed beneath his scrutiny, yet a fierce determination surged through her. Agatha would not be daunted by him or by her uncertainties. She had made her choice and now had to see it through.

"Let me see if I understand you perfectly, Miss Woodville," he said, his voice low and almost mocking. "You want to auction your virgin pussy for a sum of five thousand pounds."

Heat scorched Agatha's cheeks. "Yes." Rebecca had confirmed gentlemen of the *ton* gambled away higher sums in a single night.

He stared at her, still impassive. "I never knew there existed cunts so remarkable as to make a man pay such a price for a single night."

"Ten nights," she corrected quietly. "He can do whatever he wants, however he wants. Is that not a powerful inducement for such a reward?"

His brilliant green eyes darkened with

disbelief. "Ah ... it is your sweet innocence that makes you offer something so foolish."

"Ten nights is too long?" she asked, her voice faltering.

"For such a fortune, a man will feel entitled to do many unspeakably obscene things to your body, things you cannot even begin to imagine in your innocence." He paused, his gaze unwavering. "What are your boundaries?"

Her heart jerked in her chest. *Boundaries?* "I ... I don't know what they are, my lord."

His stare grew more intense, studying her like she was a puzzle he needed to solve. "Given your answer, I assume you have no experience with men?"

Agatha felt a sharp thump of panic. She swallowed, her throat tight. "No."

"How little?" His voice was firm, but there was an edge to it now.

"I am a virgin, my lord."

"One can be chaste but explore many other things."

She hesitated before answering, "I've never even been kissed. My hand ... a man held my hand once on a walk."

He stilled. "*Fuck.*"

The low, harsh curse sent another wave of heat across her face.

"Have you ever played with your pussy or touched it?"

Goodness. His gaze drifted below her belly, and understanding of what 'pussy' meant rushed through her. "Only to bathe."

The earl turned sharply from her, striding toward the fireplace and leaning heavily on the mantel as he stared into the flames. Agatha bit her lip, the weight of the silence pressing down on her. She knew her success in this endeavor rested entirely on this man. Madam Rebecca had been certain that Lord Radbourne was the only gentleman who would respect her body and choices in a place like *Aphrodite*.

Desperation twisted in her gut, and for a moment, she wanted to plead with him to understand. But she could only wait, watching his tense, broad shoulders and hoping he wouldn't send her away.

CHAPTER 4

Agatha braced herself as the Earl of Radbourne turned to face her. His expression was inscrutable, and his gaze was as piercing as ever.

"I will help you."

She blinked, shock rippling through her. Delight surged, so overwhelming that she nearly asked why he had decided to help her. But she stopped herself—his reasons didn't matter. What mattered was that he had agreed.

His voice, calm and steady, cut through her whirling thoughts.

"There are lessons you'll need to learn if you wish to flourish here. To know your boundaries, it's best to explore them before you find yourself caught off guard, forced to do something you don't want and something that will hurt you."

Agatha's breath hitched as a flood of

emotions surged through her. His words showed an unexpected concern for her safety, leaving her surprised and unsettled. She had expected coldness or detachment, but this ... this was kindness, and it disarmed her. Such compassion had been rare in her life, and she wasn't quite sure how to process it.

"Thank you, my lord," she said softly.

"There's no need for thanks," he replied, his tone firm but not unkind. "Each time we meet, I will test a boundary. You'll learn how to recognize and hold them. You will also learn how to flirt, how to read a man's desire, and how to balance your innocence with just the right hint of carnality. Listen to how I speak and pattern my accent. Do you understand?"

"Yes." Agatha swallowed, feeling a strange fascination rising within her. The promise of control—the ability to determine her limits—gave her a sense of empowerment she hadn't expected or thought about. That she was so naïve was a cause of mortification, but she wanted to learn. "I understand," she said, her voice steady as she nodded.

"If at any point you are uncomfortable with something," he added, his voice softening, "tell me. We stop the moment you feel it's too much."

His gaze held hers, the weight of his promise

lingering between them. Agatha felt a sense of safety, however fleeting, in those words. The situation was still overwhelming, but for the first time, she felt she wasn't entirely at the mercy of the world around her and her desperation.

"I agree," she said, her heart pounding as the enormity of what she had just committed to settled over her like a heavy cloak.

"I will touch you," Lord Radbourne said, his voice low and steady.

"I know."

"You will touch me."

"I know."

"I will teach you to be comfortable with pleasure but understand—auctioning yourself to a gentleman does not guarantee it will be pleasurable. Let me know if you would rather not learn the difference."

Agatha hesitated, her mind racing. "Allow me to answer that at a later time."

He gave a single, measured nod. "Under no circumstances will I put my cock in you. You will, in that regard, remain a virgin for the night of your auction."

She nodded, her throat tight. She almost asked what a cock was, but the words stuck in her throat, her cheeks burning with embarrassment. His gaze sharpened, and amusement flickered in his eyes for a fleeting moment before he looked away.

"I agree."

"Good. Some men's cocks are larger than others, and some men are rougher in their bed play than others. I can use my fingers to ensure your body is used to penetration, and you will not bear too much pain on the night you hand yourself over. Or, if you wish, I will not use them. What do you prefer?"

A most peculiar sensation unspooled low in her belly at the thought of his fingers on her. *God, what is this feeling?* "Would ... would they know?"

"In my experience," he said drily, his gaze gleaming. "Many men have no notion of determining if a lady is chaste. However, my touch might rid you of a virginal barrier, or it may not."

Some of her misery and doubt loosened its knot. "I want to be as prepared as possible to feel less pain on the auction night."

The corner of his mouth lifted in acknowledgment and his stare unexpectedly felt like a hot, delicate touch kissing over her skin.

"We'll start tomorrow, Miss Woodville."

Agatha lowered into a curtsy. "Thank you, Lord Radbourne."

He made no reply, and she quickly turned,

practically fleeing the room. The door clicked
shut behind her, and she found herself face-to-
face with Madam Rebecca, who was pacing the
hallway.

"Did the earl agree?" Madam Rebecca asked,
her voice eager.

"Yes," Agatha said, still trying to steady her
breathing.

The madam clapped her hands, delighted.
"Miss Woodville, we will have a very successful
future working together."

Agatha met her gaze, her voice firm. "Once
the auction is over, I will be leaving. I have a
family waiting for me. That is the only reason I
am here."

Madam Rebecca hesitated for a moment,
then gave a slow nod. "As you wish."

Just then, a young servant girl hurried down
the hallway, her steps quick and efficient.

"This is Molly," the madam said with a wave
of her hand. "She will be your lady's maid. She'll
style your hair and ensure you're dressed suitably
for your lessons. Molly will show you to your
room."

Molly curtsied briefly, her gaze warm and
polite. "This way, Miss Woodville."

Agatha followed the young maid up the
grand staircase to the fourth floor. As they
ascended, she couldn't shake the feeling that her

life had taken an irreversible turn tonight. She felt thrilled yet equally dreadful, knowing her life would change in ways she could barely imagine. But there was also something else—a strange sense of anticipation that she hadn't expected. For the first time, she felt she might hold the reins of her own fate.

At the top of the stairs, Molly led her down a long, dimly lit corridor until they reached a door at the end. The maid opened it, and Agatha stepped inside, her breath catching in surprise. Her chambers were far more luxurious than she had expected. Tastefully furnished, the room was elegant without being overly ornate. The delicate robin's-egg-blue wallpaper was complemented by drapes of the same hue, adding a softness to the space. A large bed, draped in rich fabrics, dominated the room, while a vanity with a gilded mirror stood against one wall. An armoire was in the corner, and by the fireplace, a chaise longue invited relaxation. A soft fire crackled in the hearth, casting a warm glow over the room.

Agatha stood in the center of the room, momentarily overwhelmed by the unexpected beauty and comfort. It was nothing like the sparse conditions she had grown accustomed to.

Molly hovered by the door. "Is there anything you require, miss?"

Agatha shook her head, offering the girl a small smile. "No, thank you."

After a polite curtsy, Molly left Agatha alone in the quiet, dimly lit room. She stepped over to the vanity, her fingers brushing over the smooth wood as she tried to gather her thoughts. The sheer gown Madam Rebecca had provided earlier felt far too revealing now, even though Agatha had become somewhat accustomed to its feel against her skin. A small part of her wanted to change into the cotton nightgown she had brought with her, to wrap herself in something familiar and modest.

But she dismissed the thought almost immediately. *No. I need to get used to scandalous things.* Agatha slipped out of the sheer gown and laid it carefully over the back of a chair. Then, with a deep breath, she climbed onto the bed, the cool sheets brushing against her bare skin. Lying naked, she stared up at the canopy, her mind spinning with all that had happened and what lay ahead.

Have you ever played with your pussy or touched it?

Her heart squeezed. She took a steady breath, her hand drifting to rest lightly on her abdomen, fingers inching lower with an unhurried curiosity. Her heart tapped insistently, and an unfamiliar, tantalizing ache pulsed low in her belly, settling between her thighs. Agatha frowned, letting her fingers pause atop the delicate curls that shielded her sex, acutely aware of a sensation she'd never experienced—a restless, almost aching need.

The earl's words hinted that ladies sometimes touched themselves for reasons beyond mere necessity. She bit her lower lip, and a quiver stirred through Agatha's belly as she lowered her fingers, slipping past the soft barrier of curls. She touched her sex gently, gasping—a soft, startled sound that felt foreign, as if it had escaped from someone else.

An almost intoxicating warmth unfurled, coaxing her hand into a slow, exploratory glide over her folds. Each delicate touch seemed to provoke an awareness that set her nerves alight. The ache in her belly deepened, and it felt like a sharp pull, almost pleading for more. Her heartbeat quickened, and her breaths grew shallow. Then, after a trembling pause, she let her hand fall to her side, rolling onto her belly. Her nipples brushed against the sheet, the subtle friction awakening her senses anew, leaving her both astonished and curious by this discovery.

I will touch you.

The low murmur of the earl's words teased her. Was this how he planned to touch her?

Agatha's body flushed, and she buried her face against the pillow.

This is just the beginning.

Agatha would do what she needed to do, and she would learn. She would survive. She would save her family and provide well for them. She would allow the earl to touch and explore her body, doing whatever was necessary to teach her the art of seduction. There was no fear at the notion but a deep sense of curiosity, one that both terrified and thrilled her.

CHAPTER 5

As Thomas rode in his carriage, he couldn't help but feel an unexpected measure of amusement mixed with a curious anticipation. Miss Woodville had certainly been ... expressive. Her wide eyes and the way her blushes crept up her cheeks gave away every thought she had. Normally, he found it tiresome when women feigned innocence or tried to hide their more wanton desires behind demure façades, but Agatha was different. She was too open, too transparent with her feelings. It made him wonder if that vulnerability would serve her well or lead to her downfall.

The carriage rolled to a stop in front of his home. Thomas stepped down, adjusted his coat, and strolled toward his townhouse, his thoughts lingering on Miss Woodville and how he would teach her to distinguish what she liked from what she didn't.

The hot slide of lust that swam through his veins made him scowl. This reaction was unpardonable. Still, having never done anything like this before, the idea of teaching her sparked a challenge he hadn't anticipated. Would she learn quickly? Or would she get so skittish her plan would tumble around her?

Thomas had never taken a virgin to his bed before. Hell, he doubted he ever properly kissed one. Perhaps he should ask his good friend, the Duke of Basil, who had married last year to a young lady who had undoubtedly been innocent. As Thomas opened the door and crossed the threshold, he was greeted by a piano's soft, haunting strains drifting from the music room.

He frowned, removing the pocket watch from his jacket, tilting to the pale moonlight to read the time. It was after midnight. Walking down the hallway, he encountered his butler, carrying a brandy decanter. The older man's stoic expression didn't falter as he approached.

"Master Ronald asked for something strong," the butler explained in his usual, steady tone.

Thomas paused, feeling a sudden tightness in his chest. His younger brother rarely asked for anything beyond tea or hot chocolate.

Something was wrong. "I'll take it," Thomas said.

He took the decanter from the butler and continued down the hall. Opening the door to the music room, Thomas stepped inside to find his brother seated at the piano. Ronald's short, stubby fingers glided over the keys with precision and grace, pouring his heart into the music. There was a deep, raw passion in how he played—an intensity that belied his simple, childlike nature.

Thomas walked over quietly, placing the decanter on the nearby table and sitting beside his brother on the piano bench. The melody slowed, then stopped altogether as Ronald sighed and looked up at him with those wide, round eyes. Without a word, he leaned his head against Thomas's shoulder, seeking comfort.

"Does Mother know you're here?" Thomas asked softly.

Ronald, five and twenty, was four years younger than Thomas, but his mind was that of a child. He had a kind, round face, and his eyes always carried a sweetness that endeared him to everyone who knew him. But his body had grown into that of a man, even if his mind hadn't kept up. Years ago, a physician had explained that while Ronald's body would continue to mature, his mind would remain at the level of a child. The family had been devastated, but their love for Ronald had never wavered.

That love sent a sharp lance of concern through Thomas now. How had Ronald gotten here on his own? Why had he left their mother's townhouse without anyone noticing? "How did you reach here?"

"I walked," Ronald said proudly, lifting his head. "I remembered the way the carriage took when it brought me here, so I walked from Berkeley Square to my second house."

Thomas felt his heart tighten and once again asked, "Did Mother know you left?"

Ronald hesitated, then shook his head. "No. I did not tell her."

"Why not?"

Ronald glided his fingers over the keys. "I was upset."

Thomas frowned. "Why were you upset?"

His brother's expression darkened, the usual lightness in his face dimming. "Mother was having dinner with her friends, and I asked for a glass of wine. But one of her friends said ... said only real men drink wine." His voice cracked, and his round eyes filled with hurt. "He said I am not a real man because I do not drink or attend balls or ride a horse."

A surge of fury, cold and fierce, welled up inside Thomas. The thought of someone belittling Ronald, of making him feel less than he was, filled him with a sharp, protective rage.

"I see." Now it made sense why Ronald had asked for the liquor. It wasn't about the drink but about proving something to himself, about the pain of feeling inadequate. Thomas's jaw clenched, but he forced himself to remain calm for his brother's sake.

"You're more incredible than any of those people," Thomas said quietly, his voice firm but gentle. "Don't let anyone make you feel otherwise."

Ronald nodded, leaning on Thomas's shoulder, his frame relaxing as the tension ebbed away.

"Next time," Thomas said, "inform a servant to call a carriage for you. Do not walk alone. Don't leave without telling someone."

Ronald nodded again, his voice small when he said, "I will, I promise."

Thomas offered a reassuring smile. "Now, shall we drink?"

His brother brightened immediately. "Mama said no when I asked."

Of course, there was more to the matter, but Ronald often revealed things in stages. If Thomas asked too many questions at once, his brother might become overwhelmed and retreat into himself. Best to let him share at his own pace.

"We will only have a small amount," Thomas said, rising from the piano bench. "That way, if our mother asks, we can tell the truth, and she won't worry."

Ronald nodded enthusiastically, and Thomas went to the side table, picking up the decanter of brandy. He poured a small amount into a glass and raised it to his lips, deliberately coughing after taking a sip to show Ronald that such a reaction was normal.

He handed the glass to his brother and said, "Just a small sip."

Ronald took the glass eagerly, but as soon as the liquid touched his tongue, he spluttered, his eyes watering. "It's ghastly!" he cried, wiping his mouth. "I much prefer hot chocolate."

Thomas smiled. "Then hot chocolate we shall have."

Together, they made their way down to the kitchen. Ronald hummed happily the entire way, clearly content now that he had gotten what he had come for—and even more so at the promise of his favorite drink. Once in the kitchen, Thomas waved off a couple of servants awake and set to work himself. He fired up the old earthen stove, placed a saucepan over the flame, and headed to the cold storage room for fresh milk. Next, he retrieved hard chocolate from the pantry and some sugar for sweetness.

As the milk began to heat, Thomas stirred the ingredients together, watching the mixture come to a simmer. Ronald continued to hum, rocking back and forth on his heels, content to be in Thomas's presence. Once the hot chocolate was ready, Thomas poured it into three cups and set them on the wooden table the servants usually used. Ronald, always curious, leaned forward.

"Who's the third cup for?" he asked, eyes wide with interest.

Thomas smiled. "You'll see soon enough."

As if summoned by his words, footsteps echoed on the stairs, and their mother appeared in the doorway, worry etched into her features. But the moment her gaze landed on Ronald, her expression softened with relief. His brother immediately rushed over, hugging her tightly as if the upset from earlier had been forgotten.

"Oh, my sweet boy," she murmured, kissing his forehead. "You had me worried."

"We're fine, Mama," Ronald said, beaming up at her. "Thomas made hot chocolate!"

She glanced at Thomas, gratitude and affection clear in her eyes, before making her way to the table. They sat down together, the warmth of the kitchen and the sweet scent of hot chocolate enveloping them. They enjoyed their hot chocolate in silence. The only sound was the soft crackling of the fire in the hearth. Thomas sipped from his cup slowly, shifting his gaze between his brother and their mother, feeling an odd sense of peace settle over him. The only person missing from their gathering was his sister.

"Is Victoria well, Mother?" Thomas asked, noticing a brief sheen of tears in her eyes. He didn't need to ask the reason—he already knew it was because of the thoughtless, cruel remarks that had upset Ronald earlier.

"Yes," she replied with a small smile. "I received a letter from her today. She's asking to extend her stay in Bath with Aunt Esther."

"Bath is safe, and Aunt Esther would never allow any trouble to come to Victoria," Thomas said reassuringly. "It'll be good for her to experience all the frivolities there. She will hardly have time for it when she debuts next year."

His mother sighed, her gaze softening as she looked fondly at Ronald. "Would you like to visit Bath with me for a time?"

Ronald swallowed the last of his hot chocolate, considering her offer. "Will your friend be there?"

"Lord Powell is no longer my friend," she

said gently. "I've told him as much. He won't be visiting our home again."

Ronald's face brightened with visible relief. "Good. He is mean. I do not like mean people."

"Nor do I," his mother murmured, brushing the back of her fingers tenderly along his cheek.

Thomas turned his thoughts to the man responsible for his brother's distress. Lord Powell ... yes, the viscount with the tall, lanky frame and the unfortunate mustache that had long since fallen out of fashion. Thomas mentally placed him in the category of adversary, for he was unforgiving of anyone who treated his brother with disdain or mockery. Powell had just ensured himself a permanent spot on that list.

"What about you?" his mother asked, her tone arch. "Is this the season you finally find your countess?"

Ronald nodded eagerly, grinning. "Mama says I'll have a new sister when you marry. You are taking too long. Aunt Ester says she will help Mama find you a wife soon."

Thomas turned a cool gaze on her. "Did she now?"

"Of course," she replied, her eyes gleaming with a familiar, determined fervor. "I long for another daughter to shop with and share in our gossip, especially since you've filled Victoria's head with this notion that she doesn't have to marry—that she can lead a merry life as a bluestocking, traveling London and Scotland, drawing butterflies of all things!"

Thomas raised a brow. "And if my wife happens to be just as unconventional?"

"Oh dear," she murmured, mock horror on her face. "Another one?"

"Precisely," he drawled.

Her expression softened. "Unconventional or not, Thomas ... I hope you'll come to see the value in marriage. So, does this mean you're finally open to finding your countess this season?"

A sharp, almost exasperated smile tugged at his lips. "No, Mother, you know where I stand."

She sighed, and her eyes showed a hint of disappointment. "Thomas, life can be terribly lonely."

He chuckled. "I have you, Mother. And Ronald, Victoria, my aunts, cousins ... I could hardly feel lonely with so many."

She shook her head, a wry smile forming on her lips. "That is not the kind of companionship I mean, Thomas. A man needs a wife for his heart, body, and mind."

"Ah, that delightful companionship," he said lightly, "I can find in *many* places, and I assure you, it is quite sufficient."

His mother's cheeks tinged pink, and she

scowled, muttering, "*Scoundrel*. I sometimes despair for you."

He raised an eyebrow. "As long as you still love this scoundrel, all is well."

"You're utterly unrepentant," she said, taking a measured sip of her hot chocolate. "You've always had this maddening certainty that you're immune to loneliness—or love. Not everyone is untrustworthy, Thomas. One day, what you consider 'sufficient' may fall short. But I can see by your cold expression that my words are wasted, so I'll leave it be for now."

"I would prefer the matter remain closed for the rest of the year," he replied dryly.

She shot him a glare, and he answered it with a smile.

As they finished their drinks, his mother asked, "Ronald, would you like to go home with me or stay here with your brother?"

"Home," Ronald said without hesitation.

Thomas wasn't surprised. His brother found comfort in familiarity, preferring to stay with their mother and sister, even though he had his own chambers at Thomas's residence. Ronald had only stayed with Thomas a few times in London, always returning to the safety and routine of his mother's care.

Once the last sip of hot chocolate had been taken, Thomas rose and called for his horse to be prepared. Despite the short distance from Grosvenor Square to their mother's home, he would ride alongside the carriage, ensuring they arrived safely.

Several minutes later, he watched his mother and brother enter their townhouse. Ronald gaily waved, and Thomas lifted his hand and returned it. Once the front door closed, he wheeled his horse around and started to trot home. A wicked dart of anticipation thrummed through him. Tomorrow, the lessons with Miss Woodville will begin. He had no plan and would go as the moment, and instinct, guided him. Thomas wondered what he might learn about Miss Woodville.

Bloody hell. Again, there was a pulse of desire and curiosity about what drove her to this decision. He ruthlessly closed his mental fist and banished it from his thoughts.

CHAPTER 6

Thomas sat in his private room at *Aphrodite*, waiting for Miss Woodville. It had been a few minutes since the servant was sent to fetch her. The dimly lit room was one of the few private quarters on the fourth floor, reserved for elite clients, given more for their status in the *ton* than their frequency at the pleasure palace. It was tastefully decorated, with a large bed dominating the space, a gilded chaise longue near the fireplace, and a long sofa beside a window overlooking the busy streets below. Aubusson carpets lined the floor, while heavy drapes with ornate tassels framed the windows. Liquor carafes lined the mantel along with a decanter of fine whisky on a walnut table.

The door opened, and Miss Woodville entered. Her face, though composed, couldn't quite mask the bright blush that colored her cheeks. Thomas smirked, amused by her suppressed nervousness.

"Ah, Miss Woodville," he drawled, his tone teasing as he took another sip of whisky. "Looking very much like a mouse going to the slaughter."

She delicately cleared her throat. "It is natural to be anxious."

"Not here," he clipped. "There is no room for it. Once a path is decided, there is no room for hesitation or regret."

"I agree, my lord."

He caught the slight arch of her brow at his position, her eyes flicking briefly to the glass in his hand. Thomas was sprawled indolently on the sofa, one leg crossed over his knee, perfectly aware of the deliberate ease in his posture. Most people of the *ton* would consider this stance highly improper.

"Gentlemen come here to unwind," he began, watching her take in the room. "Only a select few have private rooms like this on the fourth floor. If one of those men wins your auction, you will be taken to a room like this for the nights won."

"Yes. Madam Rebecca explained I might see a few men on the fourth floor, and I should not be alarmed by it," she said quietly, glancing around again. "I presume those gentlemen all have private quarters like this one."

Thomas nodded. "How many nights will you allow?

Her gaze swept over the large bed, the long sofa, and the well-stocked mantel. "I shared your concerns with Madam Rebecca, and she agreed to a few changes. I've decided to set a maximum of five nights. If the bidding caps at one thousand pounds, that will grant only a single night. Once the bidding reaches five thousand pounds or over, the winner will secure five nights, no more. Additionally, the winner must agree that I won't leave *Aphrodite*'s premises; all nights will take place here. This way, I'm assured the protection of Madam, the other girls, and the guards."

He nodded approvingly. "Good. You will take him to your chamber if he has no private quarters."

"These men ... have homes. Why do they need a private chamber here?"

Thomas leaned forward, setting his glass down. "Men also enjoy a place where there's no judgment, no expectation to conform to society's notions of 'gentlemanly behavior.' Some are wedded or live with family and feel they cannot be themselves. Take how I'm sitting, for instance," he said, gesturing to his leg. "It's considered impolite for a gentleman to sit with his foot crossed atop his knee. Proper etiquette demands it be at the ankle."

"How absurd," she replied, a small smile touching her mouth.

He nearly damn well shouted that she should not smile. By God, it rendered her exquisite. Thomas glanced at the perfect bow of her upper lip and the soft, inviting fullness below, his body stirring at the thought of seeing her tongue curled around his cock.

"I tell you this so you understand that when you enter a room with a gentleman, you can have no expectations of gentleman-like conduct from him. He's not here to cater to a woman's sensibilities or uphold society's standards. He's here for pleasure and to be pleased in the ways that matter to *him*. That is what *Aphrodite* promises. He will be crude if he can, or he might be charming. Understand he is even more selfish at this place, and you cannot hope he will consider your desire, even once."

"I understand."

A small silence fell as they took each other's measures. Miss Woodville seemed less nervous.

"Take down your hair," he said softly. "Never

come to me with it pinned. It is glorious when loose, and that is how most men would prefer it."

Her hand lifted, and she withdrew the pins. Dark hair tumbled around a heart-shaped face and down to her hips, and she instantly appeared more provocative with her gently sloped cheekbones, dark green eyes and a perfect, pouty little mouth. Thomas breathed in deep and long, disconcerted and temporarily stuck for words, which was quite an unfamiliar experience for him with a woman. Somehow Thomas had imagined the impact of her beauty to lessen today.

Bloody hell.

It was his turn to clear his damn throat. Thomas arched a brow, his gaze drifting over her plain, modest gown. "Why are you dressed like that?"

Miss Woodville faltered, glancing down at her attire, which had clearly seen better days. She took a small breath, smoothing her hands nervously over the fabric.

"This ... this is what I have, my lord. I sew well and will make alterations as needed to improve the fit. My gown yesterday was a loan from Madam Rebecca until I see the modiste."

Thomas clicked his tongue disapprovingly,

setting his glass of whisky aside as he rose from the sofa.

"That won't do," he said, crossing the room to her. "I'll take you shopping for clothes—hats, stockings and everything else you need."

Her eyes widened as though the idea had never occurred to her. "*Shopping?*"

"Yes," he said, his tone brooking no argument. "The madam's modiste will likely dress you like a courtesan, designed to lure men in with obvious displays of flesh. But that's not the image you should project."

She blinked, confusion flickering in her eyes. "What image should I project, then?"

Thomas studied her for a moment, a small smile tugging at the corner of his mouth.

"I'll have you dressed like a lady," he said. "But one with just a hint of sensuality. That dichotomy will intrigue men far more than if you were paraded about like one of the ladies here. You need to be different and the subtlety of it will drive them mad."

Her blush deepened, and she glanced away, clearly flustered. "I hadn't considered that ..."

"That's why you have me," he replied smoothly, returning to his seat. "You need to stand apart. The men here expect indulgence, but they also crave something more ... elusive.

And you, Miss Woodville, will become a mystery they'll pay any sum to unravel."

She swallowed, looking torn between discomfort and fascination. Her eyes were so damn expressive, revealing the emotions dancing behind their shimmering depths to anyone observant enough to notice.

"But I don't have the money to procure such a wardrobe. Madam Rebecca said she would advance a modest sum as an investor in this venture, but I do not believe it will cover even one of the gowns ladies of high society wear."

"As it is my suggestion," he said coolly, "you will leave this to me."

Miss Woodville stared at him, her hands twisting together in front of her. After a long moment, she nodded. "I will."

Thomas smiled. "Good. We'll arrange a private session tomorrow with one of the *ton*'s most sought-after modistes."

"Please tell me how I can repay your generosity."

"There is no repayment needed."

She shook her head, a small frown pleating her brow. "This is illogical. You do not know me ... yet you are so kind."

Thomas scoffed. "I am simply a man who likes to do things thoroughly. Do not read it to be more than what it is."

"I see." She canted her head. "Thank you, my lord."

"Thomas ... call me by my name."

That delicate flush swept up her neck to her face once more. "Thomas. I ... I am Agatha. My family calls me Aga."

"Let us start your first lesson, Agatha."

She smiled and sauntered closer. "I am ready."

Holding her gaze for several moments, he softly said, "Remove all your clothes and boots. Remain in your stockings only."

Her eyes widened, and her lips parted. "My chemisette as well?"

"Only the stockings will remain."

After what felt like an eternity, she lifted her trembling fingers to her mouth and muttered, "Yes, I can do that."

He watched in sheer fascination as she began to pace, talking to herself like he wasn't in the room.

"Those statues are practically naked, and I look at them all the time. It's *perfectly* normal." She folded her arms under her bosom, her pacing growing more frantic.

Thomas leaned back against the sofa, bemused by the gentle amusement curling through him.

"There was that time I jumped into the lake!

77

I was nearly naked!" she snapped, as if trying to convince herself. "This is the same."

With a sharp turn, she faced him, her chin jutting forward in defiance of her own sensibilities. Agatha stooped down and unlaced her boots, tugging them off with hasty motions. Next, she dragged her simple, worn dress over her head, revealing stockings riddled with holes. Even the thin white shift she wore beneath her gown looked as if it would fall apart at any moment. She gripped the hem of the shift, met his gaze, and began to lift it. A sharp tremor ran through her, and her eyes widened in sudden alarm. A small squeak escaped her lips.

"Bloody hell," Thomas snarled, springing from the sofa just in time to catch her as she collapsed into a dead faint.

❦

AGATHA'S EYES FLUTTERED OPEN, her vision slowly coming into focus. The ornate ceiling of the earl's private quarters at the pleasure palace swam into view behind his shoulder. She first noticed warmth, then strong arms around her and the solid weight beneath her. Agatha blinked, disoriented, and then realized she was in the lap of the earl. A warm, clean, masculine scent teased her senses. Being this close to Lord

Radbourne, his face seemed even more dangerously striking.

He was smiling down at her, a teasing glint in his eyes. Every nerve in her body suddenly became painfully aware of how close they were. His heat, the firm line of his body, and the easy way he held her—it sent a wave of mortification rushing through her.

"There you are," he murmured, his voice a low rumble. "I feared I had scandalized you beyond recovery."

Did I faint?

Her heart sank at the realization. She quickly tried to sit up, her cheeks flaming. "I—I'm so sorry," she stammered, her anger rising at herself.

How could she have been so foolish? Fainting like some weak-willed heroine from a gothic novel?

His gaze skipped over her face, dissecting every nuance.

"Shall we try something a bit less daunting?" he asked, his thumb caressing her cheek.

Her blush intensified, but she met his gaze with as much courage as she could muster. "I'm not usually so easily ... rattled."

"No?" he said, his amusement clear. "Well, fainting certainly suggests otherwise."

She bristled at his teasing, her frustration

bubbling just beneath the surface. Still, she couldn't deny the truth—he had scandalized her. She had thought their lesson would progress much slower than stripping naked at the first one!

"However," he said, his tone shifting to something more serious, "you'll need to remove that gown."

Once again, alarm scattered her thoughts, and a soft breath shuddered between her lips.

Oh, God.

He continued. "Your blushes make you seem too innocent, Agatha. Too many men have sisters they wish to protect; they'll see you as one of them if you cling to that innocence. They need to see a woman—someone they desire, not a delicate flower they feel obligated to shield."

Her heart pounded, and she felt the blush he spoke of rising again.

"You only have a few weeks before the season closes," he said smoothly, "and if you don't change how men see you, you will lose your opportunity."

Agatha swallowed hard. She knew he was right—there was no time to waste. She had committed to this path, and if she faltered now, everything she had hoped to gain would slip through her fingers. Slowly, she nodded. "I understand."

His gaze softened slightly, though his expression remained one of calm authority. "Good. We'll take it slow, but you must be willing to push past your own limits. You must become a temptress."

She wasn't sure how she would manage this transformation, but one thing was certain—if she was going to succeed, she had to let go of her fears, even if they mortified every sensibility of hers. "I understand, and I want that."

"Hmm." That devilish gleam entered his gaze. "We will have two lessons today. The first is overcoming blushes by becoming knowledgeable."

She was mere inches from the earl, close enough to count the dark sweep of his eyelashes. The subtle scent of sandalwood clung to him, teasing her senses as she inhaled deeply, trying to steady her nerves.

"Do you know what will happen when a gentleman wins you at the auction?" His voice was low, intimate. "I'm not talking about complex fantasies, but the basic elements of how a man and a woman come together."

"I have seen farm animals ... mate in the countryside," she replied. "I've heard lewd jokes in the local tavern that say it's the same."

His lips curled into a smirk. "At its most

basic, a man will put his cock inside your ... quim."

Cock? Quim? Agatha nodded, though the heat rising to her cheeks betrayed her. The smirk deepened as if he could read her thoughts.

"I know you have no real idea what I mean," he said softly. "No need to look so studious."

Drat.

He held her gaze, the intensity in his eyes making her heart race. Slowly, he placed a hand on her knee, widening her legs. Her breath hitched, and she swallowed hard. The shift she wore only fell to her knees, and his hand slid beneath the fabric, dragging upward with deliberate slowness. Her fingers tightened against his arms, caught in the spell of his touch. Every place his fingers grazed felt like tiny pinpricks of heat, and she bit her lip to stifle the small cry building in her throat.

What is this?

His hand inched closer, the heat of his palm nearing the most private part of her body, sending waves of warmth rippling through her.

"Open your legs wider," he commanded.

It felt as if a flame had bloomed through her. Agatha's body grew languorous, moving as though it no longer obeyed her will. When Thomas's hand finally touched the soft, secret flesh between her thighs, she jolted. It was better than when her curious fingers lingered last night.

"This," he murmured, his fingers lightly grazing her through the thin fabric of her drawers, "this is your pussy. Some call it your quim. Others say cunt, cunny, honey pot, velvet sheath." His eyes darkened as he added, "Every man who lays eyes on you will want to bow before you just to sink his cock right here."

Agatha's throat felt tight, and words abandoned her. Her body thrummed with sensitivity, every nerve on edge as her heart raced uncontrollably.

"Look down," he instructed, his voice a low rumble.

She did as he asked, her gaze dropping to the front of his trousers, where she saw the unmistakable thick bulge straining against the fabric.

"That," he said, his tone heavy with meaning, "is my cock."

"*Oh*," she whispered, her voice shaky. "My ..."

"Yes." His eyes remained locked on hers. "Don't act shy. Tell me."

"My breasts," she said softly, her voice almost trembling. "They ache."

He swiped his thumb across her bottom lip, his eyes darkening further, the air between them thick with tension. She was acutely aware of his fingers teasing her sex through her drawers, the pressure faint but maddening. Every stroke sent a sharp ache building deep between her thighs, the sensation almost unbearable in its intensity.

Was this desire?

CHAPTER 7

Agatha almost reached out to touch the thick bulge in his trousers, but thankfully, a bit of good sense reasserted itself just in time.

"A man and a woman can come together in different positions," Thomas continued, his voice low and steady. "You could be on your back while he mounts you, spreading your legs and taking you."

"Taking me means putting his cock inside ... to mate."

"Yes."

Silence fell as she looked at the thick bulge at the front of his trousers, wondering at the possibility of something like that actually entering her body. Anxiety seared her, and she now understood why it must hurt. Agatha thought about the stirring of need inside her body, deducing that beyond the hurt, there is this feeling that people chased. "Go on," she murmured.

"As I said, a man can climb atop your body to claim you. Or, as you are now, sitting on my lap, I could position you to straddle my thighs like one would a horse. You can take the lead and clasp his cock, tuck it at your pussy and sink down, controlling the depth and force of his entry. Or he can be the one to sheath you on his length. He can do it in a slow glide, or he could he rough and hard. You ride him to fulfillment once he is fully inside you. Or you can start before that."

Agatha's cheeks went hot, then her throat and belly. The provocative images swirled inside her thoughts.

"I've never ridden a horse," she blurted out, her voice a little too high-pitched.

Good humor gleamed in the earl's eyes. "I can teach you to ride a horse ... or let you practice riding me."

Her throat tightened, and she cleared it quickly before responding.

"Both, please," she said, as casually as if they were discussing a stroll through Hyde Park.

"You can also go onto your knees and elbows for a lover," he continued, his tone never faltering, "arching your hips and derriere into the air while he takes you from behind. You can lay on your side, and your lover molds his body behind yours, and either lifts your legs to enter you or keeps them closed for a tighter fit. There are many varied positions."

"How many?"

"Dozens. There is a book that says there are over sixty variations."

"Goodness."

His mouth quirked. "Whatever the position, the act is often referred to as fucking, tupping, swiving, or making love."

"What do you prefer?" The question leaped from her lips before she had the presence of mind to contain it.

A decidedly devilish gleam entered Lord Radbourne's gaze.

"Fucking," he drawled, his finger teasingly moving over the crotch of her drawers.

At that moment, she acknowledged how intense her curiosity about him had grown. It was a struggle to drag her attention away from the heat of his touch, from the simmering tension that seemed to fill the space between them.

He shifted, leaning forward as if he wanted to smell her skin. His breath warmed her throat.

"Have you ever wondered what it would be like to be kissed?"

Agatha's breath caught. She nodded almost imperceptibly, unable to find her voice.

He lifted his head and allowed his gaze to drop to her lips, then back to her eyes, something dangerous flickering in his.

"A lady must know how to receive a kiss, as well as how to give one," he said softly, his finger tracing a delicate path along her jawline.

"And ... how does one do that?" she asked, her pulse quickening.

A slow, seductive smile curled his lips. He leaned closer. "The art of kissing," he whispered, his lips brushing the shell of her ear, "is knowing how to use it. A kiss can be a tender invitation, a fiery passion, or a promise of raw need for a hot fucking."

That wretched heat flared across her cheeks again, and she gave up entirely on trying to control her blushes.

I must look like a boiled prawn, she thought miserably.

"Do my provocative words make you feel restless," he asked, his voice a dark caress, "or is it only mortification at having your sensibilities assaulted by such crudeness?"

"I ..." she began, but her words faltered.

He pressed a soft, wicked lick to the corner of her mouth, making her gasp. "Only honesty," he urged. "That way, I'll know how to tutor you."

"I feel something," she admitted, her voice shaky. "But I don't know if it's good or not."

"Where do you feel it?"

"Low in my belly," she said, her cheeks burning hotter. "And even lower ... to my sex."

His gaze darkened. "When did you feel it? When I spoke of tender kisses?"

"I ... I'm not sure."

"Or," he continued, his tone deepening, "when I said some kisses promise the need to fuck?"

A whimper escaped her throat, and a sharp pulse of heat bloomed between her legs. She shifted restlessly, trying to escape the confusing sensations, but only succeeded in brushing more against him. His lips twitched into a knowing smile, and for the first time, Agatha felt like she was under the scrutinizing gaze of a rake—a man who knew exactly how to make her unravel.

The tension between them grew taut, like a string ready to snap. Thomas closed the distance between them, his lips meeting hers in a gentle yet insistent caress. Agatha's heart raced, her breath shallow as her eyes fluttered closed, lips parting slightly in anticipation. At first, her response felt awkward—tentative, uncertain. Agatha's instinct was to pull away, but something in the way his mouth moved over hers, so sure and commanding, kept her rooted in place.

Then, slowly, the kiss began to change. What had started as gentle and restrained began to heat, his lips coaxing hers to respond. A rush of warmth filled her, and her hesitation melted away as the kiss deepened. Her mouth moved against his, learning the rhythm, appreciating the feel of his lips.

She gasped as he gently nipped at her bottom lip, and the soft moan that escaped her shocked her. He took advantage of her parted lips, his tongue slipping inside to explore, to taste. Hot sparks of want seemed to dance over her skin. He sucked her tongue, and her moan vibrated into his mouth. It felt scandalous and intoxicating, and Agatha leaned into him, her hands clutching at his arms for support as a wave of unfamiliar need washed over her.

Her senses were overwhelmed by the sensation of his mouth, his scent, and the heat of his body so close to hers. Every touch, every movement of his lips seemed to ignite something deep inside her, and before she knew it, the kiss had flamed into something raw and all-consuming—a simmering passion that left her trembling.

Their tongues tangled wildly, and another long, low moan broke from her lips. When he finally pulled back, her breath came in ragged gasps, her body humming with a new, unfamiliar awareness. She began to tremble as his hand settled against her cheek. Her breath faltered as he tenderly traced the line of her jaw. The pad of his thumb nudged up her chin. She opened her eyes, meeting his darkened gaze, and for the first time, she understood the power of a kiss—and how wickedly alluring it could be.

His other hand, which had stayed frozen between her legs, twitched. "Is your pussy aching?"

"Yes," she said shakily.

"I want to fuck you."

It felt as if the breath had been snatched from her body. He laughed, the sound low and almost cynical.

"I won't," he said, "but my kiss communicated that, and your body answered. Do you understand?"

"Yes."

He traced the back of his fingers along her cheek, down to her throat, and across her collarbone, barely brushing the edge of her bodice. His touch was so achingly tender it sent warmth spiraling through her. Slowly, he leaned closer, pressing a gentle kiss at the corner of her mouth, lingering there just long enough for her breath to catch. The gentleness in that kiss brought a sudden lump to her throat, and her heart seemed to quiver in response.

"This is my way of telling you I desire you ... but with no expectation of taking you to my bed. I want to touch you, to taste you. Do you understand?"

She lifted trembling fingers to his mouth, her lips tingling with the memory of his kiss. Agatha hadn't known kisses could be so varied—so exquisitely tender and pleasurable. "Yes ... I want more."

His low, rich laugh felt like a heated caress over her skin. Agatha drew a steadying breath, willing herself to calm the wild pounding of her heart and the unfamiliar hunger stirring deep within. She wasn't entirely sure what more she wanted to know, but some instinct warned her to tread carefully with the Earl of Radbourne.

CHAPTER 8

Thomas gently eased Agatha from his lap, though every fiber of his body resisted the action. The hunger roaring through him felt almost unbearable—six kisses, and he had been reduced to a man of writhing need, every touch of her lips igniting a deeper ache. He could hardly believe that something as simple as the brush of her hand against the front of his trousers would push him to the edge of losing control. A surge of sexual tension gripped Thomas, so intense it nearly unnerved him, forcing every muscle into rigid self-control.

Agatha slipped from him nimbly, looking impossibly sensual in her worn, stretched shift and torn stockings. Her tousled hair, swollen mouth, and flushed cheeks only added to her allure, and for a moment, he had to fight the urge to pull her back onto his lap and keep kissing her.

"What is the next lesson?" she asked, her voice bright and eager, her wide eyes shining with curiosity and determination.

Thomas swallowed hard, forcing himself to regain his composure. The chit would damn likely laugh if she suspected that he, a man who it took a lot to arouse, felt like his cock would burst from his trousers. He stood and walked over to the mantel, his movements measured, though his heart still raced. Reaching for the decanters lined up there, he poured a glass of champagne, then brandy, sherry, whisky, and port, placing each glass carefully on the table before turning back to face her.

"You will need to learn how to drink," he said. "Yesterday, you said you do not drink."

She canted her head. "Yes."

"Many men want their lovers to indulge with them. They feel they cannot do so with their wives. Every private room is stocked with the finest liquor, and you will often be invited to partake by your lover."

Agatha blinked, her gaze shifting to the array of glasses before her. "I've never drunk before," she confessed, her tone softer now, almost uncertain.

Thomas arched a brow. "Never? Why not?"

Sadness touched her eyes, and Agatha hesitated. "My mother died when I was young," she began quietly. "My father ... he lost himself in the bottle after that. He drank to drown his grief, and the smell of alcohol has always revolted me since then. Each time I catch its scent, I'm reminded of how my father transformed—no longer a man who laughed, but one quick to anger, treating his own children with chilling indifference."

A wave of understanding tore through him, and for a moment, he didn't see her as the woman determined to seduce and conquer but as someone who had known pain and loss. He had already suspected she endured a difficult life, perhaps as painful as many of the women who worked at *Aphrodite*. A part of him softened, though he masked it quickly.

"When my father died, it was sudden. One night, he was laughing at dinner; the next day, he was gone. I drowned myself drinking for days until the scent of liquor sickened me," Thomas admitted, stiffening, unsure why he had revealed that glimpse into his life.

"It is painful to lose a parent," Agatha said softly.

It damn well was. "The drink dulls the ... pain of feeling," he said, his voice gruff.

"Just a few days, then? Or was it weeks, months ... perhaps years?"

His jaw tightened. "I let myself drown in it for five days."

She held his gaze, her curiosity unyielding. "Why did you stop?"

Thomas paused, unused to sharing anything so personal. Even his closest friends only knew fragments of his past. Finally, he raked a hand through his hair and said, "My family needed me. That was my reason."

A shadow crossed her eyes as she looked away. "My father never stopped ... not until he met Gloria years later. That my sisters and I needed him was never reason enough."

"But he eventually stopped?"

"Yes."

There was an almost fragile quality in how she turned away as if hiding her far-too-expressive face. Yet, in the proud jut of her chin, a determination shone that belied her vulnerability.

"Do you want to give this up, then?" he asked, studying her closely. "They will push, but this can be established as one of your boundaries."

Agatha's chin lifted a fraction higher.

"No," she said firmly. "I want to try and see how it makes me feel. My mother always said,

'Fortune favors the daring.' How can anyone get what they want without venturing into the unknown and taking risks? I know what I want, and I will get it."

He suspected the woman she lost had sparked that fierce resolve in her gaze. A small smile tugged at the corner of his mouth. "Let's drink."

Agatha reached for one of the glasses on the table, her hand trembling slightly. She lifted it to her lips and took a tentative sip. Thomas watched her closely, admiring her resilience. She was an enigma—a woman who blushed at his crudeness but steeled herself against challenges. As she set the glass back down, he wondered what had driven her to take such a drastic path. What fueled her determination to push through her discomfort and continue down this road?

"Why are you doing this?" he asked, his voice low but sharp with curiosity. "What's driving you to go so far?"

Startled eyes lifted to Thomas's, her emerald gaze dark with something he couldn't quite place. Her fingers curled around the stem of the glass as she searched for an answer.

"I have my reasons. I don't expect a man of your consequences to understand."

Thomas studied her, his curiosity deepening. For the first time in a long while, he found himself intrigued by more than just a woman's body. Something beyond the typical ambition of a courtesan-to-be drove her onward—something rooted in family. And that, he understood: love, duty, and loyalty to those who mattered most. He stepped closer, his gaze never leaving hers.

"Your reasons are your own; I am no one to unearth them," he said quietly.

Her breath hitched, and for a moment, he saw something—perhaps longing—flicker in her eyes before she quickly masked it, lifting her chin in that defiant way she favored. He moved to the mantel, picking up a tightly sealed decanter with a light golden liquid.

"This is champagne," he said, opening the decanter and pouring some in a delicate flute. "Ladies tend to prefer it, along with sherry."

She accepted the glass and brought it to her lips. Thomas watched as she drank too eagerly, draining the glass in one swift motion.

His lips quirked into a smirk. "Too quickly, Agatha."

She blinked in surprise before breaking into a soft laugh. It was unexpected and genuine, and he was caught off guard at its sweetness.

"I feel as if bubbles are tickling my nose, my mouth, all the way to my stomach," she confessed, pressing a hand lightly to her belly.

Thomas chuckled. "You might find it grows on you."

She met his gaze, and he noted the wonder in her expression. "I ... I rather like it."

He handed her the decanter. "Practice sipping throughout the day. The more comfortable you become with tasting champagne, the more natural it will feel when you drink in a man's company. It will also build your resistance, and you will not become intoxicated so quickly."

Agatha hesitated briefly before wrapping her fingers around the decanter's cool glass. "I will," she said softly, accepting the task.

"Now," he said, stepping back, "let's try the others."

He handed the glass of whisky to her. She took a cautious sip, her face immediately scrunching up in distaste.

"It's an acquired taste," he said. "Not for everyone."

"I can see why," she muttered, pushing the glass away.

Next came the brandy. She took a sip, and while her reaction was less severe, she still grimaced. "Better, but still too strong."

"Fair enough," he replied. "Now, try the sherry."

Her eyes brightened slightly as she brought

the glass of sherry to her lips. After taking a sip, she nodded slowly. "This one is ... sweeter. I don't hate it."

He poured a glass of port next. She took a small sip, her brow furrowing. "It's heavy," she said thoughtfully, "but I could grow to appreciate it."

"Port is strong but has a richness," he explained. "Many men enjoy it, especially after a long night of indulgence."

She nodded, then poured champagne into the flute. Thomas raised an eyebrow, watching as she took another sip, slower this time, savoring it.

A faint smile tugged at Agatha's lips. "But this ... this I quite enjoy," she said, raising the decanter of champagne slightly.

"You have found your choice. Our lessons are finished for the night."

"I shall bid you a good night, Thomas."

She stooped to set the decanter on the carpet, then gathered her dress and slipped it over her head before hastily putting on her boots. A dark wave of humor rolled through him —she was clearly doing her best to avoid looking at him. Once her boots were on, she turned swiftly, clutching the decanter to her chest as if it were a prized possession. Her movements were quick, almost as if she were fleeing the room, her emotions tucked tightly behind her polite smile.

"What did you do today?" Thomas asked, indulging his curiosity about her. Surely, learning a little wouldn't hurt.

Agatha faltered mid-step and glanced over her shoulder, meeting his gaze.

"I read," she replied, a lightness in her voice.

"For the entire day?"

"It's one of my most beloved pastimes, and I was pleasantly surprised to find that Madam Rebecca had a small collection of books." A mischievous smile curved her lips, and her eyes sparkled with something playful. "I also ventured to the second floor. I met Lady Ellen and Bea."

Thomas raised an eyebrow at that. "How did you find it?"

Her smile deepened. "Well, they were quite welcoming."

They held each other's gaze in the quiet that settled between them, and he wanted to ask her more—anything to keep her talking and close. The need unsettled him, catching him completely off guard. "Good night, Miss Woodville," he said with chilling politeness.

Her eyes widened. "I ... I shall be going, my lord."

"I'll call for you by noon tomorrow, and we'll visit the modiste."

Agatha nodded, expression considering, as if she had something more to say. Her lips parted, but after a moment, she seemed to think better of it. With a small shake of her head, she turned again, hurrying through the door and closing it behind her. Thomas stood there, staring at the closed door, his mind still lingering on the way she had smiled—half-playful, half-reserved.

Such rubbish to find her so damn compelling.

Sighing, he reached into his jacket and pulled out his watch, glancing at the time. The hands showed just after ten in the evening. He felt a pulse of restless energy thrumming beneath his skin, the quiet of the night doing little to calm it. Thomas snapped the watch shut and slid it back into his pocket. His lips curved into a faint smile. He needed a change of pace to distract his mind from the intoxicating tension that had gripped him.

He moved toward the door with long, purposeful strides, exiting his private room and descending the staircase to the lower levels of *Aphrodite*. Soft laughter and music greeted him as he approached the second floor. The hallway was lively, filled with gentlemen and ladies reveling in their evening, indulging in drink, conversation, and pleasures the outside world often forbade.

He passed through the hallway, nodding to a few familiar faces. It surprised him that Agatha had met Lady Ellen and Bea so quickly. He wondered how she was handling it—whether she had faltered in the face of their scandalous talks or if her unyielding determination had continued to carry her through.

Thomas descended the final stairs, arriving at the ground floor. The air here was thick with cigar smoke and laughter, the hum of conversation rising from the gathering of men enjoying their brandy and cigars. Several men had ladies in their laps, and on the chaise longue, Lady Ellen was riding a man's cock, her head tossed back in sensual abandon, loud cries of pleasure pouring forth. Those who had that dark, voyeuristic hunger watched their display. A part of him wanted to join in, to lose himself in the carefree indulgence for a few hours.

But another befuddling part found his mind wandering back to Agatha. She seemed reserved yet determined, vulnerable yet strong. That contradiction pulled at him, and no amount of distraction could dull the curiosity she stirred.

Bloody nonsense.

As he crossed the floor, his gaze swept the

room, taking in the scene, but nothing captured his attention for long. Thomas felt as if his friends had cursed him. Both Oliver and James had warned him that he would soon start feeling dissatisfied with the frivolities of the *ton* and the licentiousness of *Aphrodite*. He had laughed, thinking them foolish to have married and even more foolish to claim they loved their women with every emotion in their souls.

Fucking hell.

What was this listlessness plaguing him?

CHAPTER 9

The heavy scent of lavender drifted through the air, and Thomas instantly knew Lady Anna Wimbledon was approaching. She had been his lover for a few months, but both had grown bored with each other long before now.

"Thomas, darling, I'm so glad I found you. I've heard the most alarming rumor," she said, her voice laced with intrigue.

Already? He sighed inwardly.

Thomas walked over to the open terrace, dragging in the cool night air as if it might clear the listless feeling. He pulled a cheroot from his pocket, lit it, and took a slow drag. Anna sauntered to join him, leaning provocatively against the railing. She didn't wear a mask despite being a countess. Widowed twice, Anna believed her status granted her the freedom to indulge without worrying about what others thought.

"Are you not going to ask me what I've heard?" she teased, a playful pout forming on her lips, her cobalt blue eyes piercing.

"No," he replied flatly, exhaling a plume of smoke.

She huffed in mild irritation. "You can be so frustrating."

"I know," he drawled, taking another long drag from his cheroot.

"Why do I even like you?"

"There is a loveable part of me that is clearly irresistible, even when I am an arse."

She laughed, good humor dancing in her eyes. "I'm taking Lord Dawkins home with me tonight. Will you join us?"

Anna had always enjoyed sharing her bed with two lovers, but that particular thrill had long since worn off for Thomas. When he'd realized it, they had been at his good friend Oliver, the Marquess of Ambrose's house party a few months ago. Though Anna had invited him to her bed, he hadn't felt the desire to take her. He'd kissed her body, but it had left him cold, his mind wandering as Lord Clayton—another friend in debauchery—had pleasured her with fervor. Thomas had sat in the dark, watching their tupping, darkly amused because he knew someone had also been watching through the small peephole hidden throughout his friend's manor. Even when Anna screamed in ecstasy, Thomas had remained disinterested, a fact that annoyed him more than anything else. He scowled at the memory.

"Well?" she pressed, arching an elegant brow in his direction.

"I'll decline tonight, Anna."

Her eyes widened in surprise before her expression softened. "It's been a while since you've come to my bed. I miss you. I miss how we smoked and drank together afterward. Dawkins is delightful, but he does not appreciate my droll humor ... nor can he fully satisfy my needs."

Thomas sighed, the weight of her words striking a deeper chord. Anna was more than just an occasional lover—she was a good friend, someone who understood the darker side of him without judgment.

"I've been listless," he admitted, flicking the ash from his cheroot. "And now I find myself ... distracted."

"Ah, the ingénue," she said with a knowing smile. "Is it true there will be an auction in three weeks?"

Thomas stiffened. *Bloody hell!* "Who told you that?"

"Madam Rebecca announced it tonight in the larger ballroom. The air in the room changed when she did—there was palpable excitement. She's positively in her element. She mentioned privately to me that you're the one training her." Anna's smile faded into a more serious expression. "I think she said it to provoke a reaction from me."

"Nonsense," Thomas snapped, irritation flaring. "I ought to wring Rebecca's neck. She told me six weeks, not three."

He took another long drag of his cheroot, exhaling slowly as his mind raced. *Three weeks?* That was much sooner than expected, leaving him little time to prepare Agatha. His scowl deepened, his annoyance at Rebecca simmering. She'd fast-tracked the timeline without consulting him, likely hoping to create a spectacle. The woman could be devious sometimes in her need to secure her wealth.

Anna watched him carefully, her eyes glinting with amusement. "It seems the ingénue has gotten under your skin."

"Nonsense," he said icily. "I have matters to attend. Excuse me, Anna."

She inclined her head in a subtle nod of assent, then turned and sauntered away. Thomas moved through the small crowd, down the hallway and started climbing the stairs, his mood darkening with every step as thoughts of Madam Rebecca filled his mind. The timeline for Agatha's auction had been drastically shortened, and he intended to find out why. As he neared the top floor, laughter drew his attention. In the hallway, Agatha stood with Lady Bea, giggling uncontrollably.

When Agatha spotted him, her eyes widened. She covered them dramatically with one hand and muttered, "There he is, the devil of temptation. Do you see how wicked he is? I think about him, and he manifests like a specter. Do you think he can read my thoughts and know I cannot get kissing him out of my mind?"

Lady Bea tried to suppress her own laughter and whispered, "He's really there, Agatha."

Agatha blinked, her hand still covering her eyes. She peeked through her fingers before lowering her hand and swaying slightly toward him.

"Are you real?" she muttered, stepping closer. Her fingers reached out to pinch his arm as if to confirm her suspicions.

Her mouth formed a small "O" of surprise, and then she dissolved into giggles.

"How much have you had to drink?" he asked.

Lady Bea sheepishly admitted, "We drank the decanter of champagne. She only had two more glasses. I never imagined she would be so easily ... foxed. I was escorting her back to her room to ensure she did not encounter anyone who might be tempted to act the fool."

Before Thomas could respond, Agatha stumbled slightly, her balance faltering. Without a second thought, he swept her into his arms. She snuggled against his chest, sighing contentedly.

"You smell wonderful," she murmured, her words slurring slightly. "And your body is so strong and comforting."

Thomas grunted, saying nothing, but the feel of her lush curves pressed against him stirred something tender he wasn't ready to examine. He carried her through the hallway, climbing the stairs to the fourth floor toward her bedchamber, her weight light in his arms. She nuzzled against his throat, her breath teasing his skin.

Once inside the room, he lowered her gently onto the bed. Agatha propped her hands under her chin, watching him with a sensuous smile.

"You are terribly handsome."

Thomas kept his expression neutral. "Is that so?"

She reached up and lightly traced the scar that ran down his cheek.

"This makes you look like a marauding

pirate," she said huskily. "Or how I imagined one to appear."

He stared at her, unsure how to respond to such a comment.

Agatha's expression shifted to a frown. "I don't understand," she said softly. "Why did Papa get more bitter and angry when he drank? It makes me feel warm and *happy* ... I could even remove my clothes now without fainting!"

To prove her point, she pushed herself onto her knees and fumbled with her shift, but before she could get anywhere, she tumbled unceremoniously onto the mattress, laughing.

Thomas sighed, his irritation giving way to reluctant amusement. He tugged the blankets over her, tucking her in as she continued to laugh.

"Sleep," he muttered.

Almost immediately, Agatha's laughter quieted, and within moments, she drifted into a deep sleep, her breathing soft and steady. Thomas stood at her bedside, watching her for a long moment. Despite himself, a smile tugged at his lips. Shaking his head, he turned and left her room to find the madam.

CHAPTER 10

The morning light filtered through the thin drapes, casting a warm glow across the room. Agatha woke with a start, gasping as memories of the previous night flooded back to her in vivid detail. She squeezed her eyes shut, willing the images away, but they came anyway —the laughter, the champagne, and the moment she saw Bea emerge from one of the private rooms. She was striking, with dark auburn hair fashionably cut into soft curls that fell just below her chin. Her skin had a radiant golden hue, and her bright gray eyes sparkled with life.

Bea's gentleman was also dashing and handsome. She had introduced him as Mr. Brandon Armstrong. His expression had been one of unmistakable satisfaction, and Bea's cheeks had reddened under his regard, and his murmured promise that he would call upon her tomorrow night.

Agatha had blurted out without thinking, "I am so happy I'm not the only one who blushes!"

Bea had laughed, her eyes sparkling with amusement, and invited Agatha to her chamber on the second floor. There, they had sat together, chatting, sipping champagne as if it were the most natural thing in the world. Agatha remembered how the bubbles had made her feel light and giddy, her usual restraint slipping away with each sip.

At some point during their conversation, she had found the courage to ask the question that had been gnawing at her since she stepped foot in the pleasure palace. Gloria's reply had been too vague, and she wanted the knowledge from another woman.

"What was the first time like for you? Was it here at Aphrodite?"

Bea had hesitated, her expression thoughtful as she swirled the champagne in her glass. *"It was a few years ago. I fancied myself in love with a barrister and thought he would marry me. The entire affair pleasant enough,"* she'd said after a moment, but then she glanced away, her voice softening. *"But truth be told, I hardly remember anyone before Brandon Armstrong."*

Something in her tone had made Agatha

pause. Bea's voice had softened with tender affection, and at that moment, Agatha realized Bea loved Mr. Armstrong. The way her cheeks flushed when she spoke his name, and her eyes darted away as if she were ashamed of the admission ...

"Are you in love with him?"

"I love him something fiercely, but he cannot love me even if he wants to."

Agatha's heart squeezed painfully in her chest. She felt for Bea, the yearning and loneliness wrapped in those few words.

Then Bea's mood had shifted, her expression turning serious, almost sad. *"You must always guard your heart, Agatha,"* she'd warned. *"When you give your body and pleasure to a man, it is as if he steals a part of you, especially a man who cares about your enjoyment and comfort. It's easy to fall in love with a man who treats you well, but the men who visit the pleasure palace will never marry a woman from this place."*

The forlorn tone in Bea's voice had pierced through Agatha's drunken haze, planting a seed of caution in her mind. For a moment, the thought of falling in love—of giving herself over to something so consuming—had seemed impossible, something that could never touch her. But as she stared at Bea, at the sadness in her eyes, she realized it could happen to anyone.

Agatha's heart ached for her, for the pain of longing she clearly endured. Agatha had known then that despite the laughter and enjoyment each lady she met showed, despite the gilded rooms and the beautiful gowns, there was a heaviness here—a weight that each woman carried in her own way.

"I will never allow myself to be so foolish as to fall in love." Either with her tutor or the gentleman who wins her at the auction.

Bea had nodded. *"Good."*

Agatha shoved aside the coverlets as she slowly sat up. Could she do what was required without getting lost in the illusion of affection and desire? The answer was far from clear. But one thing was certain—she couldn't be swept away. No matter how tempting the idea or how warm and thrilling the sensations might grow, she had to remember why she was here.

Agatha's thoughts drifted to Thomas. She cringed, remembering her tipsy antics in the hallway, the way she'd pinched him to see if he was real, called him the 'devil of temptation,' and—oh dear—how she'd curled up against his chest, snuggling into his arms.

She groaned, burying her face in her hands. "What did I do?"

And then, a small, treacherous part of her mind whispered that she had liked it—that his scent and the strength of his arms had felt too good, too comforting. Earlier, when he asked about her day, she felt a deep longing to talk with someone without the weight of expectations. She had never been able to share her fears with Gloria or Maggie; they relied on her strength, and if she faltered, they would crumble, too. At that moment, Agatha had been so tempted to return to Thomas, to sit in his lap and talk.

Absurd and nonsensical.

Agatha pushed herself out of bed, her feet touching the cool floor. Today, her journey continued. But she would face it with a more guarded heart.

Thank you for the warning, Bea.

Nearly an hour later, a servant hastened to inform her that Lord Radbourne had sent his carriage. Dressed in one of her best gowns, Agatha gathered her composure and stepped into the waiting equipage. The ride through London was brief, and soon they arrived at High Holborn, where the streets bustled with elegant carriages, well-dressed ladies, and gentlemen strolling in the afternoon light.

As she descended from the carriage, she saw the earl framed in the doorway of a shop. He looked impeccable, every inch the powerful, commanding figure she had come to expect. His coat was perfectly tailored to his broad shoulders, and his sharp and assessing gaze held an air of quiet authority. Agatha's pulse quickened as she moved toward him, following his silent beckon inside.

Once within the shop, she was greeted by a woman dressed in a sleek, dark blue gown that perfectly highlighted her fashionable figure. Her hair was pinned up in soft waves, and her sharp eyes immediately began appraising Agatha with the keen precision of someone who had mastered their craft.

"There are no other patrons today," Agatha remarked, glancing around the quiet, luxurious shop.

"I arranged it that way," Thomas said, his voice cool and measured, his expression as aloof.

Agatha nodded, feeling a slight flutter of nerves. The modiste introduced herself as Daphne, her movements fluid as she gestured toward the plush fitting room. She led Agatha to a table to look at fashion magazines. She trailed her fingers over the pages of the fashion print, her eyes widening at seeing the stunning ball gowns on display. The colors were exquisite—soft pastels and rich jewel tones, each gown more breathtaking than the last. There was a delicate lavender gown with silver threadwork along the bodice, a deep emerald creation that seemed to shimmer in the light, and a soft blush-pink gown with intricate lace detailing on the sleeves. The high-waisted gowns were carefully arranged to give the gowns a sense of elegance and grandeur. Every detail, from the scalloped hems to the delicate embroidery, whispered of wealth and refinement.

"They are all so lovely; I could not choose!"

Agatha had never worn anything like them before. She had been clothed in simple, serviceable, plain dresses made for practicality. But here, in this private room with the finest gowns displayed before her, she could hardly believe she could wear these luxurious garments.

"How many gowns are there?" Thomas murmured.

"Seven," Agatha said, "Will you help me choose?"

"We will take all of them."

"All seven?"

"Yes."

"Surely that is too extravagant," she gasped.

The earl merely lifted his chin to Daphne.

The modiste looked delighted. "Remove your gown, dear, so I can take your measurements."

Agatha hesitated, feeling Thomas's gaze on her. He sat in a comfortable chair, a glass of brandy in hand, watching her with an intensity that quickened her heart. His posture was relaxed, but something in his eyes made her feel exposed before she'd even removed a stitch of clothing.

"Remove your gown and shift," he commanded. "Remain only in your stockings."

The modiste's face remained impassive, giving nothing away, which only made Agatha more certain that she was used to such intimate scenes. There was no shock, no discomfort— just quiet efficiency.

Taking a steady breath, Agatha slowly unbuttoned her worn gown and slipped it off, the fabric whispering against her skin as it pooled at her feet. Her hands trembled slightly as she removed her shift and thin chemise, leaving her in nothing but her stockings. She was grateful she had worn her best pair today, conscious of how the holes in yesterday's stockings had made her feel so exposed. With deliberate movements, she reached up and unpinned her hair.

She heard the sharp intake of Thomas's breath.

The heavy tresses tumbled down her back, falling like a dark waterfall to her waist. Agatha gathered some of it in front of her, letting the thick strands cover her breasts. Only then did she peek at her tutor. His fingers tightened visibly around the glass, the tension in his body betraying the calm expression on his face.

The modiste worked silently, her tape measure moving over Agatha's waist, hips, and shoulders. Agatha could feel Thomas's gaze on her, the weight of his attention tangible as the fabric that would soon adorn her body. She stood still, her bare skin prickling with awareness, knowing he saw everything—the curve of her waist, the flush rising along her neck, the faint tremor in her fingers, the globes of her buttocks and her thighs.

A few gowns that previous clients had failed to collect were altered to fit her on the spot. Thomas had her feet and hands measured, and the modiste called her assistant from the back room, who went to another shop to purchase boots, gloves, and other fripperies. When she emerged from the private room, she was garbed in a lovely rose-colored, high-waisted gown. New stockings hugged her legs, and a charming bonnet perched atop the chignon Daphne had helped her arranged. Agatha could hardly recognize herself in the mirror's reflection.

Thomas's gaze swept over her once, a flicker of approval in his eyes, though he said nothing about her transformation. The modiste assured them she and her team of seamstresses would have the gowns ready in three weeks, and they left her shop.

"Madam Rebecca announced the auction is in three weeks," Thomas clipped. "She claimed to change the date as the season is drawing to a close, and many of the gentlemen she wishes to attend will withdraw to the countryside if you wait beyond that time."

"She informed me of it earlier. I believe I will be ready."

"Good. My carriage will be at your disposal to take you back to *Aphrodite* or wherever you wish. I will see you in two days for our next lesson."

Agatha peered up at him. "Why not tonight?"

"I'm escorting my mother and brother to Bath," he explained, and just as he finished speaking, a carriage clattered to a stop at their feet.

The carriage door swung open, and a young man with a cherubic face popped his head through the window, grinning widely.

"Thomas! I'm heading to your home," he said excitedly before his eyes landed on Agatha. His expression changed, his eyes widening as he stammered, "She's ... she's *beautiful*."

Agatha smiled, her cheeks warming. "It's

always lovely when a handsome gentleman pays such flattering compliments. Thank you."

The young man beamed like she had given him a pot of gold.

Thomas stepped forward. "Agatha, this is my brother, Lord Ronald." He gestured to the woman sitting next to his brother in the carriage. "Mother, allow me to present Miss Agatha Woodville to you. Miss Woodville, my mother, the Countess of Radbourne."

Agatha quickly dipped into a curtsy. It wasn't as graceful as Bea's or Ellen's, but she felt she managed well enough. Ronald smiled broadly, but the countess peered down her nose with an air of detached arrogance, her gaze cool and assessing.

Agatha's stomach twisted under the weight of the countess's stare.

"Oh, is this a friend, Radbourne? You have never deigned to present a lady friend to me before, most astonishing."

Agatha flushed, suddenly conscious of how she must appear to Thomas's family. Did the countess think she was his mistress? The judgment in her eyes suggested as much. Agatha fought the urge to squirm, determined to maintain her composure despite the uncomfortable scrutiny.

"Lovely to meet you both," Agatha said,

keeping her voice steady despite her heart pounding.

The countess nodded stiffly, offering no warmth in return, and Agatha wondered what thoughts were running through her mind. Whatever they were, she knew this encounter had left an impression—one she wasn't entirely sure was favorable.

"Go," Thomas said, nodding toward the carriage. "My coachman is at your disposal. He has orders to take you anywhere you'd like in town."

Her throat tightened, but she managed to smile at the earl and the countess, dipped into a graceful curtsy, and quickly made her way to the waiting carriage, conscious of his stare on her retreating figure.

CHAPTER 11

Agatha delicately waved her hand before the mirror in her chamber, practicing the graceful motion she had admired each time the earl had made it look effortless. She had been struck by how a simple movement could appear so refined. For the past two days, she diligently practiced walking more elegantly, speaking with a crisper accent, and refining her posture. Every detail mattered.

She had made full use of the earl's carriage, taking trips to Hyde Park, where she observed the ladies of society as they strolled with poise. Agatha had studied their walk—the subtle lift of their skirts, the delicate way they tilted their heads when listening, the demure smiles they offered, never too wide. She even noted the soft, measured way they spoke, each word chosen with care, as though they were as much a part of their appearance as their gowns and parasols.

Earlier, while speaking with Bea, Agatha had noticed the spark of admiration in her friend's eyes. And when Madam Rebecca heard her adopting the proper accent and tone, she gasped in surprise. Agatha couldn't help but feel a sense of pride as she moved to the bed and lay down, glancing at the notes she had made from the etiquette books delivered to her that evening after their shopping trip. The earl had left a note, urging her to read them.

Each of the three books discussed the essential points of conduct expected of a lady in society. As she scanned her notes, Agatha smiled wryly at how much there was to remember. Some of the key points she had written down included:

-It was improper to express opinions on people and characters upon a recent acquaintance, even with a gentleman who might have won you at an auction. A lady should listen politely and never ramble.

-A lady must always walk with her back straight, her steps light and controlled,

never in haste. Walking too quickly was seen as unladylike and lacking refinement.

-A lady should never laugh loudly in public. Like everything else, laughter should be restrained, more of a polite chuckle than an outburst.

Agatha snorted. It must be tedious to be a lady of the *ton*.

-A lady must never be alone with a gentleman in a private space, as it invites scandal or assumptions of impropriety.

-While in conversation, a lady should maintain eye contact without staring too intently. A gaze too direct could be interpreted as improper or overly forward.

-When a gentleman bows, a lady should respond with a gentle curtsy, keeping her head slightly lowered to show modesty. The depth of the curtsy

depends on the status of the person she
is greeting.

Agatha pushed aside the sheaf of paper. Everything seemed calculated and controlled— every gesture, every word. The rigid structure felt stifling, as if being a lady of the *ton* was not about expressing oneself but molding oneself into a precise, narrow image of perfection. She liked the mannerisms and enjoyed the new way of walking and the elegant gestures she had been practicing. Still, she was relieved that she did not belong to that world. Adhering to such strictures would surely stifle the joy in her life.

Agatha rolled onto her back, staring at the ceiling, her mind turning over the delicate balance she needed to master—the blend of demure grace and sensuality. For the past few days, she had spent hours with Bea, practicing her walk, perfecting the art of the subtle sway. They often ended up in fits of laughter, Bea teasing her about her overly serious expression as she tried to mimic the seductive glide. Agatha had grown fond of her, and despite their circumstances, she thought they might remain friends once she left *Aphrodite*.

She ran a hand through her hair, now softer and shinier than ever. It would never have occurred to her to waste eggs as part of her hair care routine, yet that was precisely what they had done yesterday. Bea had also trimmed her nails, shaping them carefully until Agatha had been astonished by the realization that hands could be considered pretty. She had even soaked in a long bath earlier, the heated, rose-scented water soothing her aching muscles. Afterward, Molly massaged lavender oil into her skin. Smiling, Agatha clambered from the bed and went to the small writing desk to retrieve a sheaf of paper. She took a few minutes to prepare the ink and quill, then sat and started to write.

Dearest Gloria, Maggie, Sarah, Carson and Henry,

I miss you all so dreadfully. It sometimes feels silly because I only left home two weeks ago, but it's true. London is a sight to behold. Its streets are bustling with carriages, fashionable people in the latest styles filling the pavements, and lads calling out the news of the day so everyone can hear it. The city feels both immense and tightly packed, with people from every imaginable walk of life. The skies are often overcast here, and the stars are dimmer than at home. I long for the open skies and bright stars of Devonshire. Yesterday, I had a charming conversation with an orange seller whose family is also from Devonshire, and the memory of home warmed me. And the food! It may be wretched of me to mention, but I have dined on prawns in crème sauce and quail with cranberry glaze. However, I promise I shall bring you all to London soon and treat you to the many wonderful foods here. There's so much variety. Each meal brings new flavors that I never knew existed. It's a true delight, and I think of all of you with each dish I savor.

I am very close to earning a handsome sum that could see me returning home sooner than I had ever hoped. I pray all is well with each of you. Should you wish to reply, direct your letter to Aphrodite on St. James Street.

With love,
Aga

A knock sounded at the door, breaking her reverie. A maid entered, curtsying politely. "Lord Radbourne is here, miss. He summons you to his private quarters."

A spurt of good humor washed over Agatha. *Summons me?* She lowered the quill and folded her letter. "Inform the earl I shall be there in thirty minutes. Please see that this letter is delivered to my home. Afterward, please return and help me brush my hair and get dressed."

The maid bobbed her head and hurried out.

She felt an unexpected rush of anticipation surging through her. As promised, the maid returned, and Agatha settled on the chair before the vanity, allowing the young girl to begin the slow, rhythmic process of brushing her hair. Each stroke sent her thick, dark tresses cascading down her back, crackling softly with a delicate swish as it reached her lower spine. The maid was meticulous, brushing it with dozens of strokes until it gleamed and felt like silk beneath Agatha's fingers.

She closed her eyes, savoring the simple luxury. She had never thought of her hair as particularly special, but in moments like these, she understood the power of presentation—how every detail, from her nails to the subtle shine of her hair, played a part in crafting an image.

Once her hair was brushed to perfection, Agatha stood, allowing the maid to help her into a simple yet elegant gown. The fabric clung lightly to her figure, teasing the line between modesty and allure. Her reflection was a far cry from the woman who had first entered the doors of *Aphrodite*.

Agatha walked to Thomas's private quarters, her steps steady though her pulse raced with anticipation. She pressed her hands to her stomach, hoping to stop the twisting nerves writhing inside.

"There is nothing to be nervous about," she whispered, lifting her chin.

Agatha knocked gently, then entered, closing the door behind her. He stood by the mantel, staring into the fire. His jacket had been discarded, his cravat unknotted, and his hair tousled as though he had repeatedly raked his fingers through it.

He straightened and turned to face her. Her breathing quickened, and that provoking heat darted low in her stomach.

"My coachman told me you only asked to visit the park twice. There are many other sights to see."

"Time and circumstances seldom permit the pleasure of reading for long hours. I spent most of the days reading. He might have also forgotten to mention that I walked about for hours, stretching my legs far beyond the parks. Thank you for allowing me to use your carriage. It was a great indulgence."

Oh, stop, she silently wailed at her rambling.

A faint smile curved the earl's lips as he nodded toward a package on the table. "That is for you."

Curious, she stepped closer, eyeing the parcel.

"It will not bite," he said dryly.

A light laugh escaped her. "What is it?"

"Books."

She snapped her gaze to his. "For me?"

"Madam Rebecca has limited titles. I thought you might enjoy these."

Agatha picked up the package wrapped in plain brown paper, its weight revealing several books inside. "These are precious," she said softly.

Memories flooded back—her mother reading with her in the meadows or by the seaside, teaching her from their single cherished book, *Robinson Crusoe*. They had read it repeatedly during the summer when she was eight. "I will take good care of these and return them as soon as I am done."

"You may keep them."

Agatha's heart lurched and her eyes widened. "Keep them? But books are expensive."

"I have hundreds in my library."

She was astonished. "You have a personal library? And it has *hundreds* of titles?"

"Yes."

Agatha could barely imagine a shelf lined with hundreds of books, all owned by one person. She bit her lip, wondering if the earl would allow her to see it. "Thank you, your ki—"

"I am not being kind," he cut in, his tone clipped. "I have already read them."

A smile tugged at her lips, but she kept her amusement to herself.

"Are you ready for the next lesson?" he asked.

"Yes."

"First, show me what you have learned. Rebecca mentioned how hard you have been practicing and how impressed she was with your progress. It seemed several of the ladies here pitched in to offer lessons."

"Yes. However, most of the time was spent with Bea and Ellen."

"What have they been teaching?"

Agatha wrinkled her nose, hating the sudden nerves attacking her. "It is possible to entice a man from how you walk and peek at him. And the first touch against his body can communicate your intent."

"Show me."

His voice was calm but laced with something darker, more intense. Was he anticipating her touch? The thought startled her, but in a way, it felt … right.

She squared her shoulders and moved toward him. Agatha wanted to scowl. Her heart was beating too fast. She reached his side, brushing her fingers across the cravat at his throat. Agatha became aware of the closeness and heat between their bodies, the firm grip of his hand on hers, his rousing masculine scent. She trailed her fingers down to his shoulder and arm. A quick peek from beneath her lashes, as Bea showed her, revealed a faintly sardonic expression.

She frowned, sensing she was failing.

The earl moved, and his gloveless fingers at her inner elbow felt like they opened pathways of sensations within Agatha's body. She swallowed, suppressing the feeling. This is how she was to make people feel, but from the icy, detached look in his eyes, Lord Radbourne was immune to her at this moment. A blush crept up her neck to set her cheeks aflame.

"I failed," she said softly. "You are unmoved."

"Again," he said, tone clipped. "Take a deep breath. You are beautiful. You are confident ... and when you let him catch your gaze—if he cannot look away—you have captured something within him, and it is that thread you follow. Confidence has its own allure."

Agatha took a deep breath and stepped back, creating a respectable distance between them.

Confidence is alluring?

She analyzed the sensations prickling over her skin, all ignited by his presence. Even at this distance, she was acutely aware of Thomas. Try as she might, she couldn't ignore her body's reaction to him. Did he feel nothing of the sort? Was this attraction one-sided? That, she supposed, was a lesson in itself—the man who won her might not stir any feelings of want within her at all. The notion startled her, but it was entirely possible, for no one else had ever affected her as the earl did.

Agatha narrowed her gaze, studying him. What drew her so much? A humorless smile played on his lips as he looked back, and she took in his aquiline nose, fierce cheekbones, and hair dark as a raven's wing. He was uncommonly handsome, and though a ruthless strength emanated from him, she knew of his quiet patience and kindness.

Perhaps this ruthless assurance was his

unshakable confidence, a quality that made him even more fascinating.

"Oh, I see," she murmured.

His gaze sharpened with interest, and a smile tugged at Agatha's lips.

CHAPTER 12

A gatha allowed calm to flow through her body as she sauntered forward, every step infused with a gentle, seductive grace. Her pulse quickened under the weight of his gaze—intense and unreadable. The quiet room seemed to shrink around them.

Thomas tilted his head slightly, the faintest hint of a smile tugging at the corners of his mouth.

"Good," he murmured, his voice low, almost daring her. "Tempt me."

Her breath caught momentarily, and Agatha hesitated, his dark, penetrating gaze leaving her breathless. She knew this was the moment to prove herself, to demonstrate everything he had taught her—how power could be subtle yet potent. His eyes tracked her every movement, the rise and fall of his chest steady yet controlled, but there was no mistaking the hunger simmering in the brilliance of that gaze.

She stopped so close that the hem of her gown brushed over his polished boots. Holding his gaze, Agatha let her fingers trail lightly along the edge of his shirt sleeve, a fleeting touch to provoke anticipation. His eyes never left hers, darkening with interest. Agatha leaned in just enough that her breath warmed his neck, her lips barely an inch from his skin. The anticipation built between them like a tightrope.

"Like this?" she whispered, curving her mouth into a knowing smile as she teased him with her closeness.

She could feel his heartbeat quicken in the charged silence, yet his expression remained indifferent. Agatha was impressed with how tightly he held his control. Thomas's hand came up, fingertips grazing her jawline with a featherlight touch, sending a tremor through her.

"Keep going," he urged, his voice huskier now.

Agatha let her eyes drift to his mouth and parted her lips in expectation as she leaned closer. She closed the distance slowly, her lips grazing his with a teasing softness, barely making contact. Thomas exhaled sharply, his control slipping ever so slightly, and that was all the invitation she needed.

The kiss deepened as she pressed closer, her hand sliding up his chest, feeling the hard muscles beneath the fabric. His lips were firm yet pliant, responding with a hunger that matched hers. Her fingers curled into his shirt, pulling him closer as their mouths moved against each other, tongues gliding in a sensual rhythm, slow and deliberate at first, before the urgency grew.

His hand moved to her waist, fingers tightening slightly as if to remind her that, for all her progress, he was still in control. But Agatha wasn't going to let him have it that easily. She sucked his tongue as he had done hers that first night and a groan vibrated from his chest in response.

Triumph surged through her when he pulled her even tighter against him, his body hard and unyielding. She felt the heat of his want, the unmistakable tension coiling between them. Pulling back just enough to break the kiss, her lips brushing against his, she whispered, "Is such a kiss acceptable?"

His eyes darkened further, a dangerous gleam in them. "It was ... adequate."

Affront snapped through her, and she narrowed her gaze. She slipped her hand between the tight space between their bodies, brushing the back of her fingers over the hardness at the front of his trousers. Her lips curled into a wicked smile. "Adequate enough to have your cock aching."

He let out a low, amused sound. "You are right; it was more than adequate."

"I want to hear more," she teased.

Thomas touched her face. His fingertips slid over her cheek as though he enjoyed the feel of her skin. "Ah, your vanity needs soothing."

"Yes."

"My cock is hard, and my balls are aching. I know I will need a release to make it through the night."

A cold sensation pierced her chest. "You are not allowed another lover while you tutor me."

He faltered into astonishing stillness, his gaze growing indifferent. The words had ripped from Agatha before she processed the peculiar sensations wrenching through her chest. The earl stared at her for several beats, and she held his regard, waiting for his cutting words.

"Very well. I will not take another woman to my bed while you are in my life."

Startled, she stared at him, uncertain what to say. "Then how will you relieve this ache in your cock."

His smile widened. "I'll merely will it away or use my hands."

Swallowing, she stepped back, painfully aware of his gaze on her. Agatha walked to the mantel, pouring herself a glass of champagne before filling a glass of whisky for him. After handing it to him, she went to the sofa, sat down, and curled her legs beneath her.

"What am I learning tonight?"

Thomas took a healthy swallow of his whisky before replying. "Men vary in their needs and desires, just as women do. Rebecca promised her patrons that her ladies could fulfill whatever desire they owned. It is why many gentlemen seek *Aphrodite*. The fantasies that torment their sleep need an outlet, and considering her promise, they come here and pay her exorbitant fees to be satisfied. Given that we have just over two weeks, we will focus on discovering what you like ... and what you will and will not allow without swooning."

His eyes darkened slightly. "I will also teach you how to give a man pleasure with your mouth and hand. These lessons will strip away whatever sensibilities you hold on to, but I promise you will be confident and ready by the night of the auction."

A wicked thrill coursed through her as she

turned over his words in her mind. "Have you been with many of the ladies here?"

His gaze became hooded. "I have been with a few."

Agatha tilted her head, studying him. "What are your desires ... and boundaries?"

"I will not be bidding for you, so what does it matter?" he replied smoothly.

Her breath hitched, and she felt a sudden bemusement—her thoughts had not wandered along those lines. "Are you so certain you would not bid for me?"

"Yes."

The immediate answer was startling. "Why?"

"The truth might offend your vanity and sensibilities."

"I am learning to set them aside," she said, tipping her glass of champagne to her lips.

He leaned back slightly, his gaze piercing. "Pussy comes too easily to me for me to pay five thousand pounds for it."

Agatha spluttered on her drink, caught off guard.

"Such self-conceit," she managed to say, amusement creeping into her tone.

"Of course," he replied, utterly unapologetic.

She couldn't help but laugh. "You are unrepentant."

"I have been accused of it," he said, a gleam

in his eyes. Then, softer, "You have a lovely laugh."

Those words drifted over her skin like fire, unsettling her composure entirely. She delicately cleared her throat. "What are the varied desires that men own?"

"There are many. Some men enjoy binding their partner's arms and legs."

She wrinkled her nose, not liking the notion of being so helpless before anyone, especially someone she did not know or trust. "I would not allow that."

He nodded. "Some like flogging or spanking their lovers across their thighs, arse, breasts."

"I would not like that and could not suffer it to please another!"

His gaze gleamed. "Some delight in only pleasing their women, devastating their senses without receiving anything in return."

Agatha stilled. "Truly?"

"Indeed," Thomas murmured, his tone deepening. "Take a gentleman I know who visits a particular woman here—Lady Bea."

"I have spoken with her several times. Bea is delightful."

"Hmm, this gentleman seems to think so as well. He goes to her boudoir once or twice a week and presumably does not allow her to touch him. He focuses entirely on her pleasure, and when you walk past her room, you can often hear her pleading for mercy."

A dart of heat pierced low in Agatha's belly, surprising her. "If it is pleasurable, why would she beg for mercy?"

The earl smiled and rose to his feet. He refilled his glass with whisky before saying, "Follow me."

Agatha complied, trailing alongside the earl from the private room, down the hall, and down the stairs into a large open room. He gestured toward the ceiling, and she looked up, gasping. The ceiling was lavishly painted, capturing a scene that was as carnal as it was captivating: a voluptuous, naked woman surrounded by five men, each worshipping her with their lips. One man's face was nestled between her thighs, another kissed her breasts, and a third pressed his mouth against her throat. Each man seemed absorbed in tasting or touching some part of her exposed skin.

"Look at her face," Thomas murmured.

Agatha's heart raced. The woman's expression was one of pleasure, yet there was a hint of something more ... almost a grimace, perhaps.

"Is she in pain?"

"Pleasure can be so overwhelming it borders on agony," he drawled, sipping his whisky, his eyes darkening as they settled on her.

His gaze sent a ripple of heat over her skin, and she blushed at the rising desire she couldn't quite control.

The earl inclined his chin, signaling their return to the fourth floor. Agatha followed, her thoughts a whirlwind of curiosity and questions. Once they reached his private quarters, she settled on the sofa, tucking her legs beneath her. The earl poured another glass of champagne and handed it to her, her fingers curling around the delicate stem.

He sat in the armchair opposite, arching a brow as he observed her. "What are your thoughts about this one? A gentleman with this desire might bid for you, and he might win."

"Are there many men here with this ... need?"

"The gentleman I mentioned seems to enjoy this weekly."

Agatha suspected he was referring to Mr. Armstrong. "If he wants Bea so much ... why would he bid on me?"

"He does not only visit Bea. Every Wednesday, he picks Lady Ellen."

Goodness. "I see."

"And he is not the only man with such desires. Many like to see their women come undone."

Are you one of those men? Agatha's breath hitched at the errant thought. "Perhaps I could set a boundary where the gentleman must comply when I say stop?"

"You could," Thomas said.

"But you do not think it is wise."

"Yes."

Her fingers tightened on the glass. "Why?"

"It is practical," he replied, "but you will lose half the men who might bid for you. Setting boundaries is important, but saying 'stop when I ask' is too broad. That leaves too much to interpretation. They could pay hundreds of pounds for you, and, at the slightest provocation, you call the night to a halt. Your boundaries *must* be specific—tell them clearly what is off-limits. Say, 'I do not wish my arse to be spanked,' or 'I do not want to be taken from behind.' If you dislike feeling pleasure without consent, make that known. But it must be clear."

"I understand," she whispered, heat pooling low in her belly. "I need to discover if ... I like any of those things to set boundaries without being too vague. I will lose some men, but not nearly as many."

A wicked gleam flashed in his eyes, his lips curling into a slow, sensual smile. "Exactly."

"Thomas?"

"Hmm?"

He tilted his head, the gleam in his gaze growing darker, more charged. He seemed to know already what she wanted to say.

"Come now," he drawled, his voice dripping with temptation. "Do not go shy on me."

Agatha emptied her glass of champagne in one swift motion and met his gaze. "I invite you to devastate me with pleasure."

His lips quirked, and he stood, exuding control and sensual promise. "Accepted. I will not stop even if you scream and beg. I will only stop when I feel I have given you enough."

A helpless surge of heat blossomed through her body. "I understand."

His gaze never wavered from hers as he issued his command. "Remove all your clothes ... leave only the stockings. Then sit on the sofa, place your feet flat onto the cushion, open your knees and let me see your pretty pussy."

CHAPTER 13

Agatha's heart raced so fast she felt faint. Gathering her composure, she stood and quietly removed her gown and undergarments, leaving herself bare except for the silken stockings delivered that morning. Delicate lace held them in place at her thighs, emphasizing the softness of her skin. She moved to the edge of the sofa and slowly sat, her movements deliberate as she shuffled back, pressing her spine against the cushions. Taking a deep breath, she drew her legs upward, placing the flat of her heels on the cushion, the subtle tension in the air crackling as she positioned herself before him.

God, she was so exposed that she felt the air on the folds of her sex.

He walked over and peered down at her. A blush engulfed her, but she did not look away from him. Agatha belatedly realized that being in Bea's and Ellen's rooms and seeing them walking around undressed had helped her.

Thomas bent over her and kissed her mouth with a feeling of almost violent tenderness. His tongue stroked against hers, and she moaned, curling her fingers into the fabric of the sofa. He consumed her, and it was as if she tasted his lust, the dark flavor of want blending with whisky. It was a short, hard kiss, and he pulled away from her, his lips softening to a tender caress that lingered at the corner of her mouth.

How could he appear so carnally domineering and gentle at the same time?

The earl lowered to his knees. His eyes collided with hers, and he held her gaze. He placed his hands atop her knees and gently nudged them wider, baring her sex to his heated stare. Agatha blushed at the hungry look that appeared on his face. She instinctively tried to close her knees, and he placed firm pressure, widening them even more. Thomas slipped his hands to her hips, pulling her buttocks to the edge of the sofa.

Oh, God.

This was far too indecent. Her sex was open to his greedy gaze, and he stared at Agatha as if he planned to devour her. Swallowing tightly, she almost protested that perhaps she had chosen the wrong lesson.

"Such a pretty pussy," he murmured.

His evocative words sent fire down her spine to land hotly in her belly. Her entire body blushed. He used the back of his fingers and brushed over her flesh. Her sex ached, sending tendrils of warmth up through her abdomen. Agatha did not understand how such a simple touch made her shift with restless need. His fingers slid through her curls, finding her nub.

Clitoris.

That was what Bea called it when she tried to discuss the anatomy of a lady's body yesterday and how they found pleasure.

He lifted his hand to her mouth and pressed his thumb against her lips. "Suck it."

Agatha's belly tightened, and she parted her lips and sucked his thumb into her mouth, holding his gaze. He dragged it from her mouth, keeping a light pressure on her lips. Thomas carried that glistening thumb down to her sex and started to rub that sensitive nub, the pressure slowly increasing. Delightful sensations began to spiral. Over and over, he rubbed, and she dug her fingers into the sofa, feeling the wetness now slicking his thumb.

She made an incoherent sound, and heat seemed to bloom from where he touched, moving to her belly, where it tightened into a hot coil. Agatha shifted her hips to ease the friction, crying out when he pressed his thumb harder against her nub. Sharp spikes of sensation pierced her clitoris and arced up her belly to her nipples.

"Place your legs over my shoulders."

Agatha complied, slipping her legs upward over his shoulders. He glided those fingers down, and he slid one deep inside her body.

Oh! The feeling of his finger inside her sex was more pleasant than she'd anticipated. He dipped his head and flicked his tongue over her navel. Her belly quivered. Thomas started to slowly stroke his finger inside her quim, so slow it felt like torture as he drew forth her wanton response. Hot need welled up, and she shifted restlessly, wanting more.

Another kiss on her belly, and he dragged his mouth over her skin and down her mons. Agatha moaned, the anticipation twisting through her body almost felt desperate. Thomas slipped a second finger inside her sex. She flinched at the tight, almost painful stretch, a groan slipping from her. His thumb somehow still found her nub, and Thomas began rubbing that delicious spot rough and hard.

He stroked his fingers inside her pussy, his thumb tormenting her clitoris with each glide and retreat. Heat spread through her, and sweat started to slick her skin. Agatha bit her lower lip, wanting to arch into him, wanting more, unable to shift, for she was pinned against the sofa, her legs high over his shoulders. She could not move, only accept the sensual assault against her senses.

"Thomas," she gasped, feeling a hot thrill of pleasure building from her clitoris, rushing up to her belly and breasts.

He leaned forward, the move sinking his fingers deeper and kissing up her body to capture her nipple between his teeth. It was as if each action added a precise increase in pleasure when she thought it could surely not feel better. He sucked her nipple, rubbing the tight nub of nerves between her thighs until she could feel the wetness soaking his fingers.

Agatha's breathing came in short pants as sharp bursts of pleasure snapped through her body. Delight rushed over her senses, washing over her in an unrelenting rush.

"Oh, God," she gasped, tremors cascading through her.

At that moment, Thomas dragged his mouth from her breasts down her quivering belly and flicked his tongue over her swollen, sensitive clitoris before sucking it into his mouth. For a wild moment, it was as if all the air had been snatched from Agatha's body, and then she found her voice to cry out at the unexpected wash of ecstasy. He licked and sucked gently, then with too much passion. She was helpless against the desperate sobs of need that escaped her throat. He drove her to madness with his tongue and fingers, and there was nothing she could do but take it. This time, the release slammed into her like a boulder. Agatha wailed as it felt like her body had broken apart.

He watched her, his expression calm, yet the piercing brilliance of his gaze told her of his hunger.

"Again," he murmured.

Her heart jerked. *Surely not.*

His fingers pinched her sensitive nub, and another wild cry ripped from her when he began rubbing it hard. Oh, God, she tried to draw back her hips but could not move.

"Thomas," she gasped. "Please ... oh, *please!*"

"Please, what?"

Her gaze snapped to his. "I feel so sensitive. It is too much!"

"I want every last drop of your pleasure."

It *was* too much. But then that aching hunger started to build again, a piercing heat low in her belly, the rising pressure and the feeling of soreness where his fingers stroked in and out, slow and gentle, then with an alternating deep rhythm. Agatha whimpered, "I feel sore. Thomas ... no more."

"Oh? Do you command me?"

The muscles of her sex burned, and a sob hitched in her throat. "No."

"I have been teasing your cunt with only two fingers. If I want, I can add a third ... a fourth."

Oh, God, not three or four! She already felt so stretched.

As if he knew her thoughts, a smile touched his mouth, and the cruel sensuality carved within his features made her grow impossibly wetter. Thomas pushed a third finger inside her sex, and she wailed. He lowered and licked her clitoris, and her body started to tremble.

Agatha burned, sweat trickled down her breasts, and she lifted her hips helplessly against his wicked mouth as he tugged her clitoris between his teeth and lashed it with his tongue. Her pussy grew sore until she rode the edge of pain, yet somehow the pleasure kept increasing. It felt as if a creature of pure carnality opened inside of her, for she tried to lift her hips, wanting more. Lust felt like a dark tide of hunger as it rolled through her, far more intense than anything felt before. Sensations nearly peaked in her belly, the tightness ready for release, but each time Agatha came close for that release to pour through her, Thomas changed the rhythm or the pressure. "Thomas, please!"

He lifted his head, his mouth wet. "I think a fourth finger, hmm?"

"*Thomas!* No—"

He dragged his thumb over her clitoris and pressed down. Sweat slicked her skin, and desire rushed through her like molten lava. Agatha's body convulsed from the sharp waves of sensation, and another shattering release broke her apart. Her vision blurred, and for a moment, she thought she would faint. With a dazed sense of shock, she realized her face was wet with tears.

His thumb moved from her over-stimulated clitoris. Thomas used his other hand to stroke her stomach before trailing his fingers down from her quivering belly to the inner flesh of her thighs in soothing sweeps. Agatha whimpered, not understanding why she felt so empty and needed more. She gasped when he withdrew his fingers from her body and slid them up to the top of her slit, pinching her small pearl. Another shockwave of sensation shuddered through her body.

"Thomas," she gasped, her clitoris so sensitive and stimulated she was almost afraid of his touch.

He used the back of his fingers to gently

brush the tender opening of her sex, which ached.

"Shh, you are doing fine," he murmured, his heated breath whispering over her mons, making her belly quiver. Then he dragged his tongue over her nub and sucked it into his mouth. Fingers wet with her release once again slipped inside her, moving slowly, while his mouth ate her pussy with decadent greed.

"*Please*, Thomas!" she cried, trying and failing to calm the arousal building through her, trying to regain a minimum of control of her own body.

Agatha was only faintly aware of her fingers gripping the cushions above her head, fevered pleas for more and then no more ripping from her throat. Her thighs trembled. Desperate to stop it but wanting more, she lowered her hands to his head, threaded her fingers through his hair and yanked. The devil did not move. When she writhed, trying to escape his erotic assault on her pussy, he sucked her clitoris with a harsher pull and worked his fingers deeper.

Agatha felt the ache ... that sweet, almost agonizing tension swell and grow low in her belly while the soreness inside her sex increased. Hot, wicked thrills of pleasure washed over her body, and she started to shake as her climax drowned her under waves of agonizing bliss. Being pushed to her absolute limits was undeniably intense and soul-shattering.

Her body still shook, and soft sobs escaped her. Thomas brushed his mouth over her shaking thighs with a tenderness that brought a lump to her throat. He lowered her legs and stood. The intensity drained from his face as if it had never been there. Was he so unmoved by everything that had just happened? Was this merely another lesson to him? Agatha shifted, her gaze catching the tension in his posture—the rigid way he held himself—and the unmistakable hardness pressing against the front of his trousers. His cock was a solid, undeniable bulge.

Thomas took two deep, measured breaths and released them slowly. The air between them was thick with unspoken tension.

"Will forced pleasure be a no for you ... or a yes?" His voice was low, tight with restraint.

"Yes," she whispered, her voice barely audible. Yet a part of her denied the notion of being with another man so.

His gaze snapped to hers, sharp and dangerous, and for a moment, Agatha was certain he would drag her beneath him and take her, all control forgotten. But instead, he clenched his jaw.

"Go," he said, his voice tight with effort. "We will resume tomorrow."

Agatha didn't hesitate. She rose from the sofa, quickly gathering her shift and gown. Dressing with trembling hands, she stole one last glance at him before rushing from the room, her heart pounding, her thoughts tangled in the storm of emotions he had stirred.

Agatha nearly collided with Bea in the hallway, her eyes wide as she glanced back at Thomas's door.

"Bea!" she said, caught off guard.

Bea's mouth quirked into a teasing smile. "It sounded like a rather ... educational lesson."

"You could hear me?" Agatha choked out, heat rushing to her cheeks.

Bea laughed. "Oh, I think half the hallway might have caught a hint! It sounded utterly delicious. A pity I never had the opportunity to experience him myself."

Agatha blinked, a strange, twisting feeling unfurling in her chest. "You ... wanted to experience Lord Radbourne?"

Bea tilted her head, a mischievous glint in her eyes, but her expression softened as she took in Agatha's reaction. She grabbed Agatha's arm, pulling her into her room before anyone could overhear. Once inside, she shut the door firmly behind them.

"What is it, Bea? Why did you come into my chamber?" Agatha asked, attempting to shrug off the growing discomfort. She winced as she moved toward her bed, a reminder of her lesson's intensity.

Bea's eyes narrowed in concern. "Did he ... well, did Lord Radbourne take you? Is that why you are sore?"

Agatha groaned and sank onto the bed, burying her face in her hands. "How am I ever to conquer these wretched blushes?"

Bea laughed and climbed onto the bed beside her. "Maybe he didn't take you, considering you're still able to sit without flinching."

Agatha gasped, propping herself up on one elbow. "And what does that mean?"

Bea wrinkled her nose playfully. "Hettie once mentioned that he's, well ... rather well-endowed."

"Well-endowed? What does that even mean?"

"You know," Bea lowered her voice conspiratorially, "his ... plug-tail is thick."

"What in God's name is a plug-tail?"

She made a sweeping motion over her mons. "You know, the earl's manroot. The things that go into our ... quim."

"*Manroot?*" Agatha burst into laughter. "*Plug-*

159

tail? The earl called it something else entirely, thank heavens. I'd have died if he'd used that term!"

Bea's laughter joined hers. After a moment, her friend's expression grew thoughtful. "You were jealous, weren't you? When I mentioned about experiencing Lord Radbourne?"

Agatha hesitated, a lump forming in her throat. Was that the feeling that hooked inside her chest? The truth settled heavily within her. She nodded slowly. "Yes ... I suppose I was. I feel rather silly. The earl is only my tutor."

Bea regarded her warmly. "It happens. I do not think feelings are things we can control. Ellen says we can."

Agatha's curiosity flickered to life. "Did you ever feel that way when Ellen was with Mr. Armstrong? Were you ever jealous?"

"At first, I was utterly seething with it," Bea admitted, her cheeks flushing as she giggled. "I even cried, which seems excessively silly in hindsight. Ellen caught me, and that's when she confessed that Mr. Armstrong only ever plays chess with her when they meet. He's kept up this entire charade to ensure no one suspects how truly taken he is with me."

"Oh," Agatha murmured. "He goes to such lengths to hide his feelings?"

"Yes," Bea sighed, her gaze softening. "I

asked him once why he bothers with the ruse, and he admitted he doesn't want anyone— especially Madam Rebecca—to know the depth of his affection."

Agatha hesitated, a pang of something unresolved tightening in her chest. "What if ... what if he bids for me?"

Bea's eyes widened in surprise. "I hadn't thought of that. You are very beautiful. There is nothing I can do about it if he does. It would hurt, but I must understand that Bran ... Mr. Armstrong is not mine."

Agatha reached for Bea's hand, squeezing it reassuringly. "If he bids and wins, I will not let you down. Once we're alone, I would suggest a quiet chess game to let Mr. Armstrong know I'm aware of his secret. He'd understand immediately that I know, and to preserve his ruse, he'll likely not expect anything of me."

Bea chuckled, shaking her head. "Devious. I see Lord Radbourne's influence on you."

They laughed and chatted, lingering longer in each other's company before Bea excused herself. Taking her friend's advice to heart, Agatha rang for a heated bath. Once it was prepared, she entered the large copper tub, savoring the warmth as she soaked.

The sore feeling instantly lessened, and she relaxed, easing the tension from the day. Nearly an hour later, she curled beneath the covers of the bed, her mind drifting to the earl and the wicked pleasure he'd introduced her to. A shiver skated down her spine, though she fought the undeniable pull he seemed to have on her.

I must not allow myself to become entangled, she silently whispered, her heart aching with the unwelcome memory of jealousy that had bloomed earlier.

CHAPTER 14

I t was illogical, but Agatha found herself craving a kind of revenge. She couldn't comprehend how her own body had yielded to such excruciating pleasure—pleasure that left her trembling, vulnerable, and still aching for fulfillment after a night of restless sleep. What stung even more was the knowledge that the earl had maintained his control while she had been utterly undone. It gnawed at her, the thought that he had reasserted command over himself while she had spiraled into sensation. She wanted to unravel him the way he had undone her.

"Let me see if we understand," Ellen said slowly, sharing a conspiratorial glance with Bea. "You want to know how to drive Lord Radbourne to the brink, to make him suffer with pleasure?"

"Yes."

Bea chuckled softly. "Oh, darling, after your lesson last night, do you wish to challenge the earl? He seemed to be a master at forced pleasure and of himself. No lady here has ever made him lose any sense of himself. Radbourne has never been enamored of anyone, and if a lady seemed to like him too much or became clingy, he dismissed her."

"There's no chance he'll dismiss me. As my tutor and a man of honor, he'll see his commitment through to the end."

"You seem to know him well," Ellen said, canting her head to study Agatha.

"I know only what he shows me," she said.

"Have you considered that might turn the tables on you again for another lesson? Not only the fourth floor will hear your pleas for mercy."

Agatha's cheeks flushed, but she held her ground. "Perhaps."

"There are so many ways to torment a man using only your mouth." Bea leaned in, her gaze gleaming with mischievous delight. "You must learn to draw out the anticipation, tease him until he is desperate for more."

"How?"

Ellen's smile widened, her voice dropping to a sultry whisper. "Start slowly ... kiss him in places he does not expect, perhaps the hollow of his throat, just beneath the ear. Men are sensitive there, more than they care to admit. Light, feathery touches with your lips, never rushing."

Bea frowned thoughtfully. "The earl has bedded neither Ellen nor me. However, he has been with Hettie ... and she mentioned though he is a giving lover he is also ... cold and indifferent to her touches. She never made him lose control, and whenever she tried, he merely smiled with that mocking humor in his eyes. Lady Susanna then took up the challenge and failed miserably."

Oh! "Bloody hell," Agatha whispered.

Ellen smiled—a sly, almost dangerous curve of her lips. "I think you should still try."

"I agree," Bea added, her eyes dancing with devilish amusement. "Tell him you want to see and understand the male body. You want to ... touch and be familiar so you are not scared."

"I like that," Agatha said, smiling.

"Take this chance to touch him all over, all for education purposes, of course," Ellen said. "Trace his skin with your tongue, the curve of his jaw, the hollow of his collarbone. Let your breath be warm against his skin, but never too much contact. Make him want it—make him beg for more."

Agatha's pulse quickened as the image

formed in her mind, the tantalizing power of turning the tables, making him lose that iron-clad control he seemed to wield so easily.

"And when you finally reach his cock," Ellen continued, "take him into your mouth, slowly, agonizingly slowly. Do not rush to please him. Every flick of your tongue should be deliberate, as if you are tasting him, learning him. Let him know you are in control."

Bea leaned closer, her voice a velvet caress. "Make him feel every single stroke of your lips, every gentle scrape of your teeth. Vary your pressure—sometimes soft, sometimes firm—but never too much at once. And when he thinks he cannot stand it anymore ... slow down. That is the real torment."

Agatha felt a rush of heat surge through her at their words, thrill and anticipation swelling in her chest. There was a wicked satisfaction in imagining herself in that role—teasing, tormenting, making him come undone.

Even if she failed, she would feel better for trying.

"And when you know he is close," Bea added, her lips curving into a sly smile, "pull away. Make him ask for it. Make him beg. That is where the power lies, darling."

Ellen nodded in agreement, her eyes glittering with amusement. "The moment you have him at the edge, that is when you will see just how easily control slips away."

The thought of driving Thomas to that brink, of seeing him struggle to hold onto his composure, made her pulse race.

"I will make him beg," she whispered.

Yet there was another part of her that simply wanted to give him pleasure. Agatha shied away from that awareness.

Both women grinned, their eyes gleaming with approval.

"We can teach you all the ways a woman can use her mouth to tease, torment, and unravel a man like him. Believe me, it's an art," Ellen murmured. "But we cannot promise it will work."

"I will—" Agatha began, determination blossoming through her when a sharp knock interrupted.

The door swung open to reveal Madam Rebecca standing with a composed smile. "Lord Radbourne is here for you, Agatha."

Astonished, she shot to her feet, glancing at the clock on the mantel. "It is only noon."

Curiosity glinted in Rebecca's gaze. "It is most unusual, indeed. The earl has never entered these premises before ten at night."

With a hurried farewell to Bea and Ellen, Agatha made her way to Thomas's private quarters, warmth and another unknown emotion flickering in her chest. She knocked gently and then opened the door. As she stepped inside, their gazes met. It was impossible not to remember the overwhelming intimate details of their encounter and impossible not to blush. The low throb in her belly deepened. Her face turned scarlet. Thomas's expression, however, remained carefully composed, revealing nothing of the savage desire she had seen last night.

"I did not expect you," she said softly. "Is everything well?"

"I have a request," Thomas said, his voice measured, though his eyes were unreadable. "It is unusual, and you are free to decline."

Her pulse quickened. "What is it?"

"I have arranged to take my brother up in an air balloon this evening."

"An air balloon?"

"Yes." Thomas continued, his gaze softening slightly as he spoke of his brother. "Ronald has wanted to experience it for the last three years. He has always said he would one day find the courage to soar closer to the stars, but until now, he kept putting it off. While we were in Bath, he told me he was finally ready. The balloon ride is arranged for today at seven in the evening. He has been talking about it nonstop."

She smiled. "It sounds as if it would be a thrilling experience."

Thomas's expression grew more guarded, as if bracing himself for what he was about to say. "The thing is, Ronald ... he specifically asked for you to join us."

Agatha jolted. "*Me?*"

Thomas nodded, running a hand through his hair. "He made the request this morning. I tried to discourage him, but he was adamant. He insisted I ask you to come along. At first, I thought to pretend I had asked, but I have never lied to my brother, and I will not start now. If you are unable to join, I will convey your regrets."

Her heart gave a small flutter. "Do you want me to be there?"

His expression tightened further. "It does not matter what I want. This is about my brother."

The thought of soaring above the earth in a balloon was thrilling. But still, curiosity burned in her. "Why does he want me there? We barely spoke."

A flicker of humor gleamed in Thomas's eyes. "He said a handsome man and a beautiful woman should share an adventure like this. It seems my brother has taken quite a liking to you."

Agatha smiled, warmth filling her chest. "I would be honored to join you both."

"Thank you," he said. "But I will warn you, Ronald is ... different. He is far more than most people give him credit for, but should you treat him in any way that hurts him, you will regret it. So, perhaps you should consider carefully if you are certain about joining."

Though softly spoken, the words landed with the weight of a sharp warning. A spark of indignation flared in Agatha's chest.

"I would never treat anyone in a way that would make them feel less," she said, her chin jutting out defiantly. "Why would you even suggest such a thing?"

"I do not know you," he said, his tone chilling.

"You know enough."

"Do I?"

"Yes. Surely, you have formed an impression of my character as I have formed of yours. Certainly, I am not more discerning than you are, my lord!"

He prowled toward her, something dangerous flashing in his eyes. "Do you think because I have tasted your sweet pussy and made you gush on my fingers and tongue, I know the kind of woman you are?"

A shocking wave of arousal rushed through

her at his words, but a sharp surge of anger matched it.

"Even if you do not know me, do not judge me based on those who have disappointed you! I am my own person, my lord. Like or hate me, but do so because of what I show you and nothing else."

Her breath came in ragged gasps as she realized how close he had come. Agatha was pressed against the wall, his presence towering over her. He braced one hand beside her head and tipped her chin up with the other, forcing her to meet his gaze. Their gazes collided, and her heart stuttered. His breath was warm against her lips, and her nipples hardened in response.

A faint smile curved his mouth, though his eyes remained cold. "Are we having our first fight?"

"Yes."

Her response was huskier than she intended, her belly tightening with the tension simmering between them. Irritated by how her body responded to his proximity, she glared at him. The tight, charged air between them only intensified.

He studied her, his eyes dark and contemplative. "Ronald is different. I do not want anyone to define him because of it. Do I have unrealistic expectations? Perhaps. But he is my brother, and I love him. Once, I trusted someone deeply, and she stood by while others mocked him—she even laughed while they hurt him."

Agatha's chest clenched with horror. "Thomas ... I am so sorry."

"You are right," he admitted softly. "I should not judge you based on someone else's actions. I have enough good sense to know that not everyone is the same, and a person should be measured by their words, actions, and honor. It will not happen again, Agatha."

Her throat tightened. "Thank you.

He lowered his head in a sharp nod.

"Did you make them apologize?"

A faint smile tugged at his mouth. "When I found three supposed friends by the lake, tossing apple cores at Ronald while he sobbed, and my fiancée laughed, my reaction was immediate, brief and vicious. Everyone left with bloodied lips, and there was a broken bone. I waded in with my fists."

His fiancée?

Thomas's hand left her chin and touched the scar on his cheek. As if realizing he had revealed more than intended, his expression grew distant again, and he began to pull away. But Agatha moved with him, sliding one hand around his neck while the other lightly traced the scar on his face.

"I hope you hurt them," she murmured. "*Badly*."

"Bloodthirsty."

Her heart stuttered. "When necessary. I am very protective of my family ... I cannot imagine them being so hurt."

His lips twitched in amusement. "I have never spoken to anyone about that incident. Not even my closest friends, Oliver or James."

Her eyes widened. This admission felt like a warning—an unspoken caution that she had touched something he rarely shared, and if she were not careful with what he offered, Agatha would bitterly regret it.

His fingers grazed her cheek, then traced the delicate arch of her brow. "It was a temporary madness. It will not happen again."

"Thomas," she said, her chest warming with a peculiar tenderness. "I would never betray your confidence."

"We shall see."

The cold mistrust in his gaze was painful to bear.

"My father is obsessed with gambling," she admitted, holding his eyes and feeling a raw vulnerability she hadn't endured when David demanded to know why they were leaving

Cringleford and why she no longer wished to marry. "He owed eighty pounds and couldn't repay it. He ... he offered my younger sister in service here at *Aphrodite* to clear his debt."

He went still. "Why are you telling me this?"

Agatha swallowed, her throat tight. "Because ... I want to give you a part of myself, too. Something real."

His unwavering gaze roamed her face, yet there was a tenderness there she had never seen before. She didn't know what to make of it. Agatha wished he didn't wear indifference like a second skin so she could read and understand him better. In the few times they met, there always lingered a distant aloofness and an austereness to his expression. Agatha ... wanted to shatter it and know the gentleman beneath his cultivated, impenetrable mask.

The awareness made her heart stutter. This man before her was untouchable for someone like her, and it was utterly foolish even to entertain the thought of being drawn closer to his allure.

Thomas is only my tutor, nothing more, she told herself firmly, almost frightened by the softening she felt inside, the growing longing to sit and laugh with him.

"How did you end up here instead?" he asked, his voice quieter now.

"My ... my sister is only sixteen."

"That blackguard," he hissed. "How could he be so vile?"

The earl's distaste was oddly comforting. "I couldn't bear the thought of her coming, so I took her place. A duke settled the debt for me—without asking for anything in return. I returned home afterward, but I knew my father would gamble again. He always does."

A searing flash of awareness burned through her as she stared at Thomas, and regret unexpectedly twisted inside her. Too many emotions quaked through her heart, and she did not want this man to know how much she had wept and feared, how much pride she had relinquished to decide to auction her virginity so her family might live in contentment. She turned away, hiding her face from his steady gaze, but he didn't push her for more.

A long silence stretched between them, nearly unbearable. Then, in a low murmur, Thomas said, "I'll send my carriage for you at seven."

Surprised, Agatha looked up and found him watching her as if she were an enigma he couldn't quite solve. She nodded, then quickly turned and hurried back to her bedchamber, wondering at the imperceptible shift between them just now.

CHAPTER 15

Agatha's soft, womanly scent teased his senses in the cool night air. Thomas inhaled deeply, trapping that delicate fragrance inside his body. He felt a strange and unwelcome lurch in his chest—something he had not expected and certainly did not want. Across from him, Ronald gripped the edge of the air balloon's basket, vibrating with excitement, and Agatha mirrored him, a radiant flush of wonder lighting up her features.

She looked utterly enchanting tonight, her figure draped in a deep rose-colored gown that contrasted beautifully against the twilight sky. The gown, though simple in cut, shimmered faintly in the lantern light, highlighting her every movement with grace. Her hair was pinned loosely, with soft curls framing her face.

She looked lovely and carefree, her emerald eyes sparkling as she took in the scene around her.

Several men, bundled in thick coats and mufflers, worked diligently to loosen the tethered ropes that kept the balloon anchored to the ground. The balloon was a magnificent sight—vast and gleaming in shades of blue, from pale sky to deep midnight, carefully chosen hues that Thomas knew would delight his brother. The massive canopy billowed above them like a slumbering giant waiting to rise. The hired balloonist, a gruff man with a weathered face, barked commands to his crew as they primed the valves and adjusted the flames, readying the burners for the ascent.

"We are going up!" Ronald shouted, his cherubic cheeks glowing a bright red as he bounced on his toes, barely able to contain his joy. "Aga, are you prepared?"

"I am!" Agatha let out a delighted laugh, her voice light and musical. "We are truly about to go into the sky. My mother once told me she watched an air balloon ascend here in London, and she drew so many images for me to picture the spectacle. I cannot believe that I'm *inside* one now. My sisters will be green with envy!"

She turned her gaze to Thomas as if inviting him to share in the moment. He stood at the opposite side of the basket, watching her and Ronald.

"I never imagined inside was so large," she said. "Surely, at least twenty people can fit."

"This one is a bit larger than others," Thomas murmured.

The balloon could easily hold at least thirty people, and Thomas ensured it was designed with the utmost care. The vivid blue hues of the balloon had been precisely chosen as they were his brother's favorite color.

"When are we going to start going up?" Ronald shouted, hopping from one foot to the other in his eagerness.

Thomas smiled. "Mr. Powell will soon fire the burners. We'll start floating higher when the air inside heats up enough."

"How high will we go?" Agatha asked, her voice filled with wonder.

"At least five hundred feet, milady," Mr. Powell replied with a nod. "We're about to lift off."

The ropes were untethered, and the balloon began its graceful ascent. The moment the ground fell away beneath them, Ronald let out a triumphant bellow, the sheer exuberance of his shout echoing through the open sky. Agatha startled, glancing at him in surprise, but soon laughed.

"What was that?" she asked, her eyes gleaming.

"Sailors shout 'ahoy' when they set sail," Ronald explained, his face aglow with excitement. "We're sky sailors now, so we shout, too!"

Agatha grinned, clearly amused. "That sounds perfectly logical."

Thomas watched her, bemused, the warmth in her expression softening something inside him. There was nothing pragmatic about her laughter or Ronald's exuberant logic, but Thomas kept his counsel. To his surprise, Agatha tipped her head back and let out a loud, joyful holler into the night sky—a sound so raucous and unladylike yet so free and alive that it struck him as impossibly lovely. This encouraged Ronald to shout more, and even Mr. Powell did not seem to know what to make of the scene.

The balloon soared higher, the world below shrinking away as the cool wind kissed their faces. The vast expanse of the London skyline stretched beneath them, the gasp lamps twinkling like scattered stars, while above, the real stars shimmered in the deepening dusk. The sensation of floating weightlessly in the sky, with nothing but the basket beneath their feet and the vast canopy of the balloon above, filled the air with quiet magic.

Thomas, despite himself, felt the thrill of the moment settle in his chest. Agatha stood at the edge of the basket, tendrils of her hair catching the wind, her face tilted to the stars, and he found it impossible to tear his gaze from her. She was radiant, her joy infectious, and for a fleeting moment, Thomas allowed himself to be swept up in the same sense of wonder that had overtaken her and Ronald.

Despite all the times he had soared in a hot air balloon, it had never felt quite like this. Perhaps it was the company he shared in this moment that filled him with a bewildering sense of contentment.

"We're flying," Agatha said, her voice filled with awe.

His brother slowly nodded as if he could hardly process the experience.

"I cannot believe we're flying," Ronald murmured. He glanced over his shoulder at Thomas. "Brother, we are *flying*."

THE BALLOON RIDE was nothing short of magical. Standing near the edge of the basket, Agatha marveled at how the London landscape slowly shrank beneath them, the varied lights of the city twinkling like scattered jewels. Above, the sky stretched endlessly, the stars breathtakingly beautiful in the velvety expanse. The gentle sway of the balloon and the cool wind against her skin made her feel weightless and free in a way she had never imagined.

One day, she would take Gloria, Maggie, Sarah, Carson and Henry to experience this and other sights in London. Agatha would save diligently for it. Awareness rippled under her skin as Thomas moved closer to his brother. Ronald had brought a small brass telescope, which he held tightly to his eye as he scanned the horizon with childlike wonder.

"I can see so far," he gasped.

"What can you see?" she asked.

"*Everything!* The city, the river, the lamps and fireplace in people's windows, and I think ... yes, I can see the stars better from here. They're so bright."

Agatha smiled, a wistful ache piercing her chest. "It's like we're flying among them, and there is a feeling that if we go close enough, we just might unravel the wonders of our world."

She lifted her hand toward the sky, narrowing her gaze and peering up, making it appear like the stars were resting delicately on the tips of her fingers. "I wished we could go closer."

Ronald nodded, seeming beyond words. He lifted the telescope toward the stars again, captivated by the view.

Agatha turned to Thomas, who had remained quiet, watching his brother with deep affection. "You are quiet."

His gaze flicked to her, and so effortlessly, her heart skipped and danced beneath her breastbone.

"I have been in an air balloon several times."

"This very one?"

"No. This was one specially made for Ronald."

"This ... it is owned and not rented?"

He glanced at Ronald. "When Ronald and I were younger, we often climbed trees together. My brother always wanted to do what I did, even when it was hard. We sat on branches for hours, staring at the stars. We talked endlessly about the possibilities of this world—that maybe, just maybe, life existed somewhere beyond the stars. He believed that is where our father went, and I agreed. Whenever he was troubled, we would climb a tree and talk."

Agatha tilted her face toward the sky, captivated by the idea. Such thoughts had never occurred to her before. Life, for as long as she could remember, had been about surviving—how to make it through the day, the week, or the month. It was always about ensuring there was enough food for her siblings, blankets to keep them warm, or finding help when they fell ill. There was never any room for whimsy ... or friendship, or dreams.

Since her mother's death, Agatha realized she had not stopped moving or worrying. She did not dwell on the past or allow herself the luxury of imagining the future. She was firmly rooted in the present, each moment consumed by responsibility.

What would it be like to imagine, even for a moment, that the distant dreams she once held inside could come true?

A tight sensation gripped her heart as the thought took hold. What would it be like to have someone in her life who encouraged her to reach for those dreams—someone who would catch her and hold her close, even if she never quite achieved them? She swallowed against the unfamiliar feeling that stirred within her, an unknowing longing that felt terrifying.

"What happened after?" she asked softly, the question almost an invitation to understand something she had never known.

"He told me he wished he could be closer to

the stars. I promised him that one day he would be."

"From that conversation, you had this built?"

"Yes," he said, gazing at the sky. "It took time, but I wanted to be sure it would be here for him when he was ready."

"But ... what if he never wanted to take the ride?"

Thomas didn't respond right away. Silence stretched between them, the only sounds being the faint creaking of the basket as the balloon drifted higher and Ronald's occasional sigh of happiness.

Finally, Thomas spoke, his voice quieter than before. "It wouldn't matter. It wouldn't be a waste. I just needed him to know that the opportunity was there if he wanted to explore."

Agatha stared at him, her heart swelling with an intangible emotion that vanished before she could understand its existence.

"You are wonderful," she said, her voice barely above a whisper.

Thomas jerked slightly, his eyes snapping to hers. For a moment, he stared at her, then his mouth quirked. The man before her seemed so different from the whispers that echoed through the halls of *Aphrodite*. Many claimed he was a disreputable libertine; some even called him cunning and dangerous. They spoke of him as a reckless gambler, capable of losing thousands of pounds in a single night, only to win it back and more. Some ladies said he had no feelings of softness or whimsy, only cold pragmatism. However, Agatha realized they did not know the man, only what he allowed them to see. She wanted to know him.

"Come here, Agatha."

The low command sent a ripple through her. She glanced at Ronald, still absorbed with the spyglass pressed to his eye, eagerly scanning the skies and horizon.

"When he gets lost in his own world, he can ignore everything around him for hours," Thomas murmured. "I have often wondered what it would like to live in his thoughts."

Agatha stepped closer, her movements slow and deliberate. She maintained a respectful distance while infusing her steps with a subtle, practiced sway that conveyed sensuality.

A wicked gleam lit up his eyes. "Ah ... you're putting your lessons to use, I see."

She tilted her head, smiling slightly. "How is my walking?"

"Sensual and provocative, just as it should be. Balanced perfectly with a touch of coltishness and grace—enough to catch the eye without seeming too practiced. It's enough to tempt any man to forget himself."

She laughed, absurdly delighted. "What do you enjoy ... other than flying in hot air balloons?"

"There is no mystery as to what brings men enjoyment."

She inched closer so her words would only reach his ears. "Unfortunately, I am not well-versed in the pursuits of men of consequence like yourself."

"All men are the same."

Agatha sniffed. "Country gentlemen tend to their farms, take long walks in the woods, and share their troubles with their cows. I once saw Mr. Baddon complaining to his heifer about the grief his wife gave him. The cow seemed startlingly understanding and *mooed* at all the right moments. I cannot imagine you having this chat with a cow. Do you even have cows, my lord?"

Thomas laughed, the sound warm and rich, sending butterflies fluttering in her belly.

What is this feeling?

"I like quality whisky, carriage racing, sailing my yacht on the open seas, gambling ... and fucking, though making love has its own pleasures." He raised his brow, that devilish glint deepening. "How easily you blush."

Agatha let her lips curl into the soft, carnal smile Bea and Ellen had taught her. "I was merely thinking that I now understand the delights of ... *fucking*, thanks to your recent lesson and quite understand why it is a source of delight."

He went still, his gaze sharpening as she let her fingers drift softly over his arm, the touch barely there. This was meant to be another lesson of subtlety in the art of seduction, but as her fingers lingered, she realized it was more than that. She wanted to touch Thomas—not to provoke a response or gauge his reaction, but to be close to him. The thought unsettled her, and she briefly closed her eyes, wrestling with the unfamiliar ache that stirred within her.

Agatha lifted her lashes and met his regard. "I am quite certain there is more to you, and I'd like to know more if you will allow it."

His hooded eyes swept over her, an unfathomable guardedness in his gaze.

She brushed a wisp of hair from her cheek, aware of the sudden tightness in her heart. "If you have no wish to share, I do understand."

An almost irritated grunt slipped from him, and he looked toward the horizon. They sailed in the air for several beats before Thomas murmured, "I enjoy my family."

That peculiar thrill scythed through her heart. "What about them?"

"My brother sees life with an innocent

wonder. Sometimes ..." The corner of his mouth curled into a faint smile. "Sometimes, I talk with him to remind myself that there are still beautiful things in the world worth cherishing. My sister, Victoria—she's a hellion at heart. It shatters my mother's nerves, but I want her to stay exactly as she is. And my mother ... she's quick-witted, clever, owning an indomitable strength I only understood after my father's death."

Thomas stroked the tip of his finger along the skin below her chin, his touch sending warmth through her.

"What do you enjoy, Agatha?"

"Are you truly curious, or is this mere politeness, my lord?"

"I am not a man who subscribes to niceties," he drawled, his voice laced with amusement. "I don't ask out of obligation."

Agatha smiled. "I enjoy reading."

"Is that all?"

She hesitated, her gaze drifting to the glistening water in the distance. From this distance, the Thames looked almost serene, masking the filth that usually sullied its surface.

"I don't really know what I like," she admitted quietly. "I have never attended the theatre, Covent Gardens. I want to see the fruit market there. I love oranges."

"Oranges," he said slowly as if he did not know what to make of her.

Agatha felt a sudden pang of inadequacy. He must think her so gauche. "It is silly—"

"Nothing about you is silly."

Ripples of warmth ghosted over her skin.

"You like oranges. I like grapes," he said. "What else?"

Agatha was unequivocally flustered by the intent yet tender way he regarded her.

"I also enjoy spending time with my family."

His steady gaze held hers, unblinking, as though he were absorbing every word. It made her self-conscious, and she laughed nervously.

"I ... would like to visit the Royal Opera House, Vauxhall Gardens, or the Royal Museum. Bea and Ellen said that these are wonderful places to explore. I do enjoy long walks ..." Agatha paused, another soft laugh escaping her lips. "And I've recently discovered that I quite like bathing in rose-scented water."

"If you could pick one thing to do tomorrow," he asked, "what would it be?"

She blinked, startled by the question. No one had ever asked her such a thing. Agatha scowled. "You will be responsible for the expectations rising inside me, my lord. You must ensure they are met."

Thomas chuckled. With a sense of

bemusement, she realized that she liked hearing him laugh.

"Pick going to a ball," Ronald said suddenly, his voice cutting through the conversation.

Agatha spun around to face him, surprised by the suggestion. He was still fixated on the spyglass as if the night sky held answers to the world's greatest mysteries. "A society ball?"

"Yes," Ronald answered, lowering the glass just enough to flash her a wide, enthusiastic grin. "My brother can do anything."

Her heart stuttered at the certainty in his voice. Such unshakeable faith in another person ... she could not imagine it. Agatha shook her head, turning back to Thomas.

"That was never in the realm of my expectations. A *ton* ball would be too grand for me."

"Pick a ball," Ronald urged before returning to his telescope. "Brother does not like attending balls because mama always asks him to marry a lady from there, but I know he will take you without hesitation."

Agatha was astonished. "He *would?*"

"Yes," Ronald said, "you are his friend."

Her gaze collided with Thomas's, and there was a most perplexing hope in her heart that she was afraid to examine.

"Would you like to attend a ball?" Thomas

asked, his voice softer now, as though genuinely curious.

The very idea of it made her heart race with a strange sense of excitement. The grandeur, the elegance—she could barely imagine it. A sobering thought struck her. "What would be the point? I do not know how to dance and would not know anyone there. Would I not be an oddity? How would I even procure an invite?"

"I thought Ronald explained I can do anything."

She glared at Thomas, and he smiled.

"I will be your partner in ... boredom for the night. There is no need to worry about knowing anyone there."

"*Boredom?*"

"Balls are excessively dull; however ... in three days, you will receive an invitation, and I will teach you to waltz within three days."

Her breath hitched. The idea of dancing with the earl—of being in his arms in such a setting—made her pulse flutter and her belly tightened in a way she couldn't explain. Agatha nodded, overcome by an emotion she couldn't quite name. Agatha's lips parted, but before she could speak, Ronald's excited voice cut through the moment.

"Thomas! Look at this!"

He turned to his brother, who was holding the telescope toward him. "What is it, Ronald?"

"I can see the entire moon, and it's *huge*!"

He took the spyglass. "Let me have a look, then."

Who are you, Thomas, and why do I so badly want to know?

She leaned against the basket and watched Ronald and Thomas. He laughed at something his brother said, then ruffled his hair. The earl was a man of deep loyalty who kept promises and built dreams, even if they were never fulfilled. And that, Agatha thought, made him more wonderful than he could ever realize. A sharp warning pierced her chest, but she brushed it aside. Tomorrow, she would reassert her good senses ... but now ... she wanted to savor the sensations blossoming through her.

It was new, scary ... and wonderful.

CHAPTER 16

Y*ou are wonderful.*

Three simple words, yet they clung to Thomas, haunting him long into the night, lingering in his thoughts as he drifted into sleep, and followed him even now as he walked into *Aphrodite*. He had been praised countless times before—flattery flowed easily in his world—but Agatha's had oddly pierced him. They were not born of obligation or a desire for favor. She was ... genuine. The taste of her pussy on his tongue lingered; the feel of her tightness around his fingers kept his cock hard for hours afterward. The memory of her trembling, her heels digging into his shoulders, her emerald eyes dark with lust as she unraveled lingered, teasing and tormenting him relentlessly. Still, the joy on her face and her laughter in the hot air balloon stayed with him even longer.

Thomas made his way through the halls of *Aphrodite*, his steps steady as he ascended to the third floor.

"My lord," a breathless voice called from behind.

It was Lady Bea, looking flustered, her cheeks flushed. Thomas arched a brow. "Yes?"

She clasped her fingers before her. "You ... you are *early*."

He tilted his head, noting the accusatory tone beneath her breathless voice. "It is seven."

"You ... you hardly ever come before midnight," she stammered. "Lady Agatha is not available."

"Where is she?"

Bea glanced away nervously. "Learning ... from Madam Rebecca. They are not to be disturbed."

Thomas smiled and strode toward the fourth floor. He approached the madam's boudoir, knocking briskly before a young maid opened the door and ushered him inside.

"No ... no... too fast, slower, more sensual ... *yes*! Now again ... yes, perfect!"

Lifting a brow, Thomas stepped into the private parlor and faltered, feeling as if his damn breath had been snatched from his body. There, before him, was Agatha, dressed in a way that seized his every sense. A small slip of emerald silk clung to her breasts, leaving little to the imagination. Her belly was exposed—the soft curve of her skin gleaming in the candlelight. The skirt, a matching emerald, hung low on her hips, and long slits at the sides revealed the flawless length of her thighs and legs. Gold beads adorned the hems of the fabric, catching the light with every slow, sinuous movement she made.

What she wore was unlike anything he had ever seen on another woman, so utterly provocative it made his heart hammer against his chest.

She was dancing.

Agatha's hands twisted gracefully above her head, her fingers trailing through the air as her hips rolled and swayed to an erotic rhythm he could not hear. Her belly undulated in a slow, sensual wave, her movements deliberate, tantalizing. It was as if her entire body was singing with a language of seduction he had never known a woman could possess.

Thomas's mouth went dry, and he could only stare, frozen in place, his senses enthralled. There was a magnetic allure to her, something raw and untamed, and it struck him forcibly that he could not move his fucking gaze away from her. He was used to controlling every situation and desire—but at that moment, she had all the power, leaving him reeling.

Another sinuous twist of her hips and their gazes collided. Agatha's eyes were half-lidded, and a small smile curved her lips, teasing, knowing. She wasn't just learning—she was becoming something more, something fucking irresistible.

You are wonderful.

Thomas scrubbed a hand over his face. What the hell was this nonsense?

Agatha moved closer, the sway of her hips never faltering. Her eyes locked on his as if she knew exactly what she was doing to him. The golden beads shimmered with each step, the soft rustle of silk filling the space between them. His body tightened with a fierce need, every muscle coiled, waiting for anything to break the tension that stretched between them like a taut wire.

Thomas clenched his jaw, willing himself to maintain composure, but the fire she ignited within him was impossible to ignore. She was no longer the hesitant, blushing girl from a couple weeks before. She had transformed into a woman who could command desire with a single glance, a roll of her hips.

"Bravo," Madam Rebecca said, "I have *never* seen such a look on Lord Radbourne's face. *Well done*, Aga."

He masked his expression and took a step forward. "You have learned well."

Agatha stopped her dance and stood before him, her chest rising and falling with the exertion of her movements, but her smile remained, teasing the edges of his self-control.

"I had a good teacher," she said softly, the heat of her gaze never leaving his. "I have been practicing for hours."

"I daresay Agatha is a natural," Rebecca murmured, a cool mocking in her gaze as she stared at him. "It took me a couple of days to reach where she is now."

Agatha laughed. "It is a dance called *Raqs Sharqi*. Madam learned it when she lived with her lover in Egypt a few years ago," she said, her voice carrying a new, sultry confidence. "I love it."

"I wanted Agatha to attend the naughty musicales I keep and do this performance to ... whet the appetite of her bidders. However, she wants to leave this for the night of the auction. The men must only know they are in for an *unparalleled* delight."

The thought of the many eyes on her, hungering to have her beneath them, filled Thomas with a raw feeling that was completely unknown.

He cleared his throat, forcing his thoughts

away from the provocative dance and back to why he had come early. "I came to teach you the waltz."

Madam Rebecca, who had been watching with mild amusement, turned her gaze on him, her brows lifting.

"Why does she need to learn the waltz?" she asked.

Agatha, her face still flushed, did a most unexpected twirl. "I am going to a society ball!"

Madam Rebecca's head snapped toward her, then back to Thomas, her eyes wide with surprise. He knew what was going through her mind—he had never mixed his life here at *Aphrodite* with his life in the *ton*. The two worlds were always kept separate. The curiosity in Madam Rebecca's gaze was palpable, but Thomas remained indifferent, staring back at her without revealing a single thought.

"I am here to teach you the waltz," he said again, "Come on."

Madam Rebecca's mouth quirked into a slight smile. "Well then," she said, her gaze lingering on him for a moment longer. "You should also play the flute for her next practice."

"I will hire a master for that," Thomas replied, his voice smooth, but a note of finality silenced further discussion. It was likely best if he wasn't present when Agatha learned this dance.

"That will be quite expensive," Rebecca said, though her smile widened as she realized what he meant.

In return, he lifted a single brow, and that was all the answer she needed. Rebecca nodded, understanding that Thomas would be covering the costs. She excused herself from the room with a light chuckle, leaving them alone.

Agatha smiled at him. "Are we going to dance here?"

"I would prefer my chambers or yours."

Her eyes flickered with curiosity, but she remained silent as they left Madam Rebecca's boudoir and walked down the hallway toward his private quarters. Her steps were slower, more hesitant, and Thomas noticed the pensive look on her face. They reached the door to his private room, and Agatha leaned back against it.

"Why are you helping me so much?"

"I already told you. I am a man who commits to a task wholeheartedly."

She frowned, her lips parting as if debating her next words. "Is that all I am to you, then? Just a cause?"

He stiffened. "What else am I supposed to see you as?"

Agatha gave a small, almost playful shrug,

her eyes holding a glimmer of something that made his chest tighten.

"Perhaps ... a friend."

It wasn't often someone tried to bridge that gap with him. He was used to keeping people at arm's length, and they, understanding his reserve, kept their distance. Tupping and friendship did not mix. In his experience, it always led to unrealistic expectations he had never promised. "Friends?"

She tucked a tendril of hair behind her ear. "Have you ever thought that you'll help prepare me to be the perfect lover ... for someone else? Does it trouble you in any regard?"

Her words hit him like a blow, a sharp, knife-like sensation twisting in his chest. For a moment, he didn't know how to respond. The thought of her being with someone else—someone who would benefit from all the lessons he had given her—filled him with a sudden and inexplicable sense of possessiveness.

"No," he said, his voice colder than he intended. "Why would it?"

"I was merely curious." Agatha lowered her lashes, her expression unreadable, before she turned, opened the door and stepped into his room.

Thomas stood there for a moment, watching her disappear through the door, his jaw tightening. The knife in his chest remained, its sting sharper than he cared to admit. But with a deep breath, he pushed it away and followed her inside. A single lamp lit the room, casting soft shadows across the polished floor. Agatha stood in the center, waiting, her hands clasped before her. Thomas shook off the unsettling feeling and focused on the task at hand.

"We're here to waltz," he said, stepping toward her.

His tone was controlled, but a hunger he did not like simmered underneath it all. Thomas approached her, placing one hand on her waist and taking her other hand in his.

"The first step is to feel the rhythm. The waltz is about grace but also connection. Follow my lead."

She nodded, her expression serious but soft, her eyes meeting his with a quiet determination. "I am a quick learner."

"First, you must always maintain this frame." He gently placed her left hand on his shoulder, firmly holding her other hand. "Your posture needs to be graceful, shoulders back, chin up. Never slouch, even when you relax."

She adjusted her posture, trying to mirror his movements.

"Now, the basic step," Thomas said. "It's

three beats—one, two, three. Think of it like a square."

"A square." Agatha frowned, glancing down at their feet.

He gave a small smile. "Yes. Step forward with your right foot for the first beat." He moved, guiding her forward. "Then, to the side with your left for the second beat."

She followed, her steps tentative but steady.

"Finally, bring your right foot together with the left on the third beat. That's the first part."

"Forward, side, together?" Agatha repeated.

"Exactly. Now, I'll move backward as you step forward. Always mirror your partner."

They began to move, and Thomas murmured, "Keep the rhythm. The key to the waltz is to let the movement flow. There should be no hesitation, only trust between you and your partner."

Agatha swayed in his arms. "How do I turn?"

"Once you've mastered the basic step, we'll add the turn. On the first beat, step forward and pivot as you go to the side. It's a gentle twist of the body." He demonstrated, pulling her closer as they turned smoothly, his hand guiding her waist.

Agatha's breath caught at their closeness, but she focused on the dance, her steps growing more confident. "Like this?"

"Perfect," Thomas said, his voice low. "Now, keep turning with the music."

Her eyes laughed at him. "It is a tad difficult without the music."

He made some low sounds in his throat, trying to imitate the hums.

She dissolved into laughter. "You sound like something dying."

Thomas smiled. He had deliberately done a bad job because he wanted to see this smile on her face and hear the joy in her chuckles. They continued dancing, gliding across the room.

"Oh, this is wonderful. I see the appeal of attending balls so often. Bea tried to explain the season, and I was astonished that some indulge in such pursuits for weeks before retiring to the country to hunt. I cannot imagine what I would do with such leisure."

Thomas lowered his head and pressed his lips to the corner of her mouth. A dark hum of pleasure blasted through him.

Agatha stilled. Her soft, wondering gasp whispered across his skin like a touch. "What lesson is this?"

Fuck. Since their first kiss, they had shared several more. Each was a lesson, with instructions flowing between every lick and nibble. He guided her through soft kisses, deep, passionate ones, and those meant to tease and tempt. But for Thomas, it wasn't just about teaching anymore. He found himself craving the press of her lips against his because he wanted to feel and taste her.

"This is no lesson," he said, reasserting his control and then drew back. "Let's continue dancing."

Agatha nodded, her steps growing lighter as they twirled together. After nearly an hour of practice, Thomas felt a simmering restlessness burn through him. He excused himself and left Agatha, heading downstairs to one of *Aphrodite's* lavish drawing rooms. The room was filled with soft laughter and the clinking of glasses as several of Madam Rebecca's ladies, all beautifully gowned, entertained gentlemen lounging in comfortable chairs and sofas. Thomas entered, still feeling that gnawing sense of discontent, but forced himself to move through the room with an air of ease.

His friend, Brandon Armstrong, lifted a brow when he spotted Thomas. He leaned back, swirling his drink, an amused look settling on his face.

"Well, well," Brandon said. "I never expected to see you down here tonight. There is a rumor going about."

"Hmm, what has Lady Bea told you?"

Brandon tugged at his cravat. "It could have been someone else."

"Unlikely," Thomas drawled. "Given your obsession."

His friend scowled. "I am not *obsessed*."

Brandon sighed at Thomas's pointed stare.

"Bea merely said you seemed ... fascinated with a new lady that will soon put her virginity on auction. Is it true?"

"I thought Madam Rebecca announced the date of the auction."

Brandon smirked. "Oh, everyone is abuzz with the notion of the auction. I am asking if it's true you are fascinated."

"No," he clipped.

A half smile touched his friend's mouth. "Fancy taking a girl or two upstairs?"

Thomas stared down into his glass, feeling empty. It was as if nothing in the room, not the laughter, warmth, or flirtatious looks cast his way, could touch him. When he searched himself for what would fill that void, the answer hit him with startling clarity—he wanted to go back upstairs—to Agatha.

"Bea surprised me by suggesting that she and Ellen—"

"I am not interested," Thomas said, his voice a little more clipped than he intended.

Brandon raised both brows this time, setting

his glass down. "Not interested? *You?* This place is your playground."

"Is it?"

"What's wrong? You seem ... *different*."

Thomas exhaled slowly. "When I figure that out, I'll let you know."

Brandon studied him for a long moment, then smiled knowingly. "I wonder if it has something to do with the new lady in your life. I can tell you from experience that it happens when one least expects it, and there is no control over these feelings."

Thomas's jaw tightened at the insinuation. He downed the rest of his drink, unwilling to entertain this conversation any longer. But the truth gnawed at him, and deep down, he knew something was different.

CHAPTER 17

Three days later, Thomas took Agatha's hand, helping her step gracefully from the carriage. The vibrant sounds of laughter and the distant strains of the orchestra echoed from Countess Rafferty's townhouse. Arriving just minutes before midnight, they avoided the receiving lines, ensuring a more discreet entrance. Agatha looked breathtaking, her light blue ballgown clinging to her figure in a way that made her seem almost ethereal. The gown shimmered under the moonlight, and the soft curls of her dark blonde wig framed her face, enhancing her already striking beauty. He watched as she lifted her fingers to the pearl necklace at her throat, remembering her shock when he'd gifted it to her yesterday—and how adamantly she'd insisted on returning the necklace and earbobs after the ball.

"Are you ready?"

Agatha nodded, her cheeks faintly flushed. "I wish Ronald were here. He said he always wanted to attend a ball."

This was a sentiment Thomas heard often; however, his brother would change his mind the moment it was time to leave. "We will bring him along next time."

Her eyes brightened, a soft smile playing on her lips. "Will there be a next time?"

Thomas hesitated, surprised by the sharp realization that he wanted to take her to all the places she longed to see. "Why not? I enjoy spending time with you."

That awareness cut through him like a honeyed blade. He couldn't quite understand why, but the desire was there to know what made her happy, sad, or worried, undeniable and unsettling. Agatha lowered her lashes, hiding her thoughts. He extended his arm, and she delicately placed her gloved fingers on his forearm. Together, they walked toward the countess's townhouse.

For the last days, their lessons had been devoted to perfecting her grace, refining her accent, learning the subtle art of flirtation, and dancing the waltz. Afterward, they would drink together, discussing the wicked possibilities of intimacy and the importance of sexual needs and compatibility. Though she could not have the choice to pick her lover, Agatha was undeniably curious, quick-witted, and so innately sensual that she often stole his reasoning. She had also become more forthright in her questions, confidently setting boundaries.

There would be no flogging, whipping, or spanking. She would not tolerate a ginger root inserted anywhere. She would not act like a governess chased and ravished by the master. She would permit forced pleasure. She would allow all manner of sexual positions.

The glint of curiosity in her eyes as they spoke had made him harder than a mere physical touch ever could. They had covered countless topics, yet her gaze still held a sweet innocence that tugged at something deep inside him.

Agatha had become dangerously good at everything, often making him lean into her allure before snapping back when she gleefully exclaimed that she'd seduced him with her newfound wiles. When her mock frustration surfaced at failing to captivate him, she'd flutter her lashes comically, and he'd laugh despite himself.

She had a sharp mind for cards, too, and the revelation that her father had taught her, using those moments to practice his card-sharp techniques, had saddened her. Agatha had real talent—she could likely win a fortune if she played at the gambling dens. But he'd seen the deep disgust in her eyes when she spoke of those places, and he understood. If it weren't for the predatory nature of the gambling halls, her father might not have spiraled into such dishonor, unable to tear himself from their grasp.

"Lord Radbourne and Lady Belladonna," the butler announced as they entered.

Agatha made a small, startled sound. "You gave me a name that's a deadly flower."

A ripple went through the crowd, and Thomas watched the visible reaction of many to her beauty. Covetous male eyes watched her all around the room, and she seemed oblivious to all.

"Goodness ... this home is magnificent," she whispered, awe lacing her voice.

The chandeliers above, adorned with hundreds of glowing candles, bathed the ballroom in a warm, golden light. Thomas knew Agatha must find it all excessive. He imagined that affording even a few candles for the year had been a struggle for her family. They strolled leisurely around the fringes of the ballroom, her hand resting lightly on his arm.

"Quite a few people seem to be staring at

you, their alarm and curiosity barely concealed behind their fans," Agatha said.

Thomas chuckled. "It has been a few years since I last attended a society ball."

"Why the absence?"

"Many assume that a bachelor's presence at these events signals he's ready to marry. I am not interested in the nonsense that comes with their assumption." His eyes landed on his good friend Oliver, the Marquess of Ambrose, and his wife Lily. Thomas guided Agatha toward them, noting the subtle tension in her posture. Only because he had spent so many hours observing her did he catch the fleeting moments of nervousness. To others, she was the picture of cool elegance, an untouchable beauty with a quiet air of hauteur.

"Thomas," Lily said warmly, her face lighting up with a smile as they approached. "It has been too long."

He did not mention that he saw her only a few weeks ago. "Lady Ambrose," Thomas said, bowing over her hand with a practiced charm. "You grow more beautiful with every meeting."

Her golden-brown eyes sparkled with humor. "You are ever the charmer."

Thomas turned to Agatha. "Allow me to present my friend, Lady Belladonna. Agatha, this is Lily, the Countess of Ambrose, and Oliver, the Marquess of Ambrose."

"Oh, how beautiful you are," Lily exclaimed, her eyes widening in admiration. "I would love to design and make a gown for you."

"You sew?" Agatha asked.

Oliver stiffened, his blue eyes flicking to Agatha in warning. A brief flash of discomfort passed across Lily's face. She perhaps thought Agatha would judge her for being a seamstress, a part of her past that society did not easily forget, even if she had married one of London's most eligible bachelors.

"I do," Lily said, her tone carefully measured. "Though I am a marchioness, it is a passion of mine. I am overseeing the opening of an exclusive boutique that ladies will shop from only by invitation. We're creating gowns more beautiful than those in Paris."

Agatha's smile bloomed, transforming her poised beauty into warm radiance. "That's wonderful. I sew, but I'm not as talented as my sister, Maggie. She dreams of becoming a premier modiste."

Lily's eyes lit up. "You sew ... and make clothes for others?"

"Yes," Agatha said with an eager nod. "But I am not skilled enough to rival those gorgeous Parisian gowns."

"I daresay I shall invite you to model my latest creation. Many will sigh with envy and send me many letters *begging* for a similar style."

Thomas exchanged a bemused glance with Oliver, watching their women engage in a lively discussion about fashion. He stiffened slightly. *She's not my damn woman.*

Still, as he observed Agatha's ease and joy in conversing with Lily, he felt inexplicable satisfaction even as Thomas rejected the reason —Agatha's contentment.

❦

AGATHA NEVER IMAGINED she would have such fun at a *ton* ball. The room was elegant, aglow with hundreds of candles suspended from crystal chandeliers. A twenty-piece orchestra filled the air with music, mingling with laughter, light chatter, and the delicate fragrance of ladies' perfumes. She felt a thrill of success throughout the night. Thomas introduced her to several people, and though some recognized her name as a fabrication, they were too polite to ask. It titillated Agatha to know she didn't belong, yet they couldn't tell, or this notion of propriety prevented them from prying. Some lifted their fans and whispered she was a mistress, and only Lord

Radbourne would dare. Others whispered she was a distant cousin, and some said she was an actress.

She laughed and charmed, and many seemed to fall under her spell. Still, it was exhausting, for the only people she could be her true self around were Thomas, Lily, and her husband Oliver. The love and tenderness in the marquess's gaze as he looked at his wife nearly made Agatha blush. That tender yearning on Lily's face whenever she stared at her husband brought a hot lump to Agatha's throat. It was a rare and beautiful thing to witness. She had been careful to avoid the main floor of the pleasure palace, but she recognized a few gentlemen in attendance tonight. One particular man caught her attention, for Ellen often spoke about him, wishing he would ask her to be his mistress.

Thomas handed her a glass of champagne. "What is that look on your face?"

Agatha discreetly lifted her chin to a couple dancing. "Is ... is that not Lord Eglinton?"

"It is."

"And his partner ... is that his wife?"

"That is indeed Lady Eglinton."

Shock sliced through Agatha. "He visits *Aphrodite* often and always asks for Lady Hettie or Lady Ellen."

"Why do you sound so surprised?"

Her fingers tightened around the stem of her champagne glass. "Are you not shocked?"

"No."

"Why not?"

"It's natural for a man to keep a mistress and have several lovers."

Agatha stared at him as if he had grown two heads. "There is *nothing* natural about dishonor," she said quietly. "You may think me naïve, but a man and a woman make a vow—a promise before God when they marry. A promise of faithfulness, loyalty, and love. If a man breaks that, he's a dishonorable bounder who deserves to rot. I cannot fathom the hypocrisy of your society—to look down their noses at others while holding such a view."

"You're right," he said with soft intensity. "That's why I've always said I'll never marry."

A nameless agitation rushed through her body. When he explained why he avoided balls, she assumed he was not ready. "You ... you don't plan to marry? Even years from now?"

A cynical look entered his gaze. "I can't imagine having just one cunny for the rest of my life, nor am I inclined to change my mind because of this mystical love that changed my friends' opinion on the matter. So, no, I will not be marrying. I have others who will inherit."

He was such a paradox. Agatha knew

Thomas had a sense of honor, yet he was a libertine. She realized that his honor kept him from marriage—so he wouldn't break his vows. A sharp ache bloomed in her chest. She took a slow, deep breath to steady herself against the emotions flooding her.

This ache, this piercing awareness that felt trapped beneath her skin, the wild flutters in her belly, and the maddening desire to walk into his arms and rest her head against his chest were aggravating reactions to this man. Whatever she felt would never be mutual, and she despised how helpless she felt, tumbling into something so unfamiliar, something she couldn't control.

The orchestra struck up, violins filling the room with an alluring melody.

"Will you dance with me?" he asked.

"Yes."

He led her to the dance floor, guiding her into position. Agatha could feel the eyes of the guests on them, but the moment his arms wrapped around her, all anxiety melted away. Her skin felt sensitized, her heart pounding as if in rhythm with the music. She could even feel the warmth of her breath trembling over her lips.

As the sensual strains of the waltz enveloped them, they began to move. Their bodies flowed together effortlessly, each step imbued with grace and quiet elegance. The earl's intensity was almost unnerving. Neither of them spoke, and Agatha was grateful for the silence—it allowed the tension between them to stretch, simmer, and deepen with every movement of the dance.

Agatha was more acutely aware of herself than ever before. Since the night he had teased and tormented her until she lost count of her climaxes, there had been no further carnal intimacy between them. Instead, over the past few days, he focused on refining her speech, how she walked, and how to subtly tease a man. A simple brush of her fingers along the lapels of a jacket, a coy smile beneath lowered lashes, leaning just close enough to tempt and then pulling away when he attempted a discreet touch—all designed to ignite desire while holding it just out of reach.

Thomas had taught her that most of the art of seduction involved denial of need, stoking and building hunger until it was unbearable.

Agatha wanted more than kisses ... and it did not feel as if it was in pursuit of lessons. She wanted Thomas. She wanted to haunt him as he had started to haunt her. Memories of the night her legs were splayed high on his shoulders, her sex opened to his debauchery would sometimes resurface at inappropriate times, catching her off guard and sending her heart racing.

Like now ...

"I would like another lesson," she said.

His mouth hitched into a small smile. "I suspect you have something in mind that you want to practice."

"Yes."

"What?"

She could feel a flush creeping up her cheeks and wished she could control her reaction. "You will see once we return to your private apartments at *Aphrodite*."

As the final strains of the waltz faded, Thomas guided her off the dance floor. He led her towards the exit, bypassing the crowd.

"Are we not going to bid farewell to Lord and Lady Ambrose?" she asked, surprised by their sudden departure.

"No."

As they walked outside, his fingers rested at the base of her spine, making her acutely aware of every point where they touched.

Once they were settled in the carriage, Agatha's pulse quickened as the temptation to crawl into his lap and kiss him simmered just beneath the surface. She longed to feel his mouth on hers, to surrender to her desires. But she resisted, her fingers curling into her dress as she held back.

The ride to the pleasure palace was short,

yet it felt interminable. When they arrived, he took her hand and led her through the halls of *Aphrodite* to his private quarters. The air crackled with expectation. Once inside, he closed the door behind them, the soft *click* echoing through the room.

He turned to her. "What lesson do you want tonight?"

She stared at him for a long moment, her heart hammering in her chest. Then, with a confidence that surprised even herself, she lifted her chin, met his gaze, and said, "Remove all your clothes ... boots ... everything. Until you are naked."

A flicker of something—desire, amusement, or maybe even challenge—crossed his face. His mouth curved into a slow, wicked smile. Thomas began to unbutton his coat, his movements deliberate, the sound of each button coming undone loud in the charged silence.

Agatha stared as he shrugged off his coat, tossing it aside. Then, with painstaking slowness, he began removing his boots, his eyes never leaving hers. Her gaze traveled over the sharp planes of his body, tracing every movement as he peeled away the layers. He undid his waistcoat, revealing the broad expanse of his chest beneath the fine linen of his shirt.

When his shirt finally joined the pile, her

breath hitched. His skin gleamed under the soft light of the room, every ridge of muscle defined and carved in perfection. He held her gaze, waiting to see if she would falter in her demand. But she didn't.

"Every flick of your tongue should be deliberate, as if you are tasting him, learning him. Let him know you are in control."

Her friends' teachings whirled in her thoughts, and she softly said, "Keep going."

He smirked, a devilish glint in his eyes, before reaching for his trousers. There was no hesitation in his movements, only confidence and an undeniable allure that sent a pulse of heat rushing through her veins.

As he stepped out of the last of his clothing, standing before her completely bare, Agatha's mouth dried. He was *magnificent*.

"Should I turn around?" he teased.

"Yes."

Thomas chuckled but complied. His thighs and calves were thick and powerful, stomach and buttocks lean and delineated with muscle. The raw masculinity of his body was overwhelming, and for a moment, she couldn't speak or move, only stare. Every inch of him exuded power, control, and an irresistible sensuality. A thick stalk of flesh twitched and increased in size under her stare.

Goodness.

Thomas arched a brow as if daring her to continue with her next command.

At her silence, he drawled. "What now, Agatha?"

"Now I practice what I have learned on you."

"Oh?"

That sound felt like a purr rasping against her sensitized skin. Her belly tightened. She wanted to practice everything on the earl, not because she wanted to know for future lovers but because he would like it, and she wanted to see him come apart for her. It was dangerous, for it pushed her closer to losing a piece of herself to him, a piece she might never regain. Agatha took a steady breath, her desire tightening inside her, and with a soft, sultry smile, she stepped closer to him, fully prepared to take control of the night.

CHAPTER 18

Who was this woman walking toward him?

Thomas became acutely aware of his heart beating in an unfamiliar rhythm. He wasn't used to being looked at this way, with tender longing and delight. He was used to greed, machinations, avarice, and lust. Not *this*. His throat tightened, and for the first time in a long while, Thomas found himself unsure how to respond. That emerald gaze felt like it was dismantling them piece by piece, and he wasn't certain he could stop it. "Agatha—"

"You shall not speak, my lord."

Bloody hell. "What lesson is this?"

She stopped walking, smiled, and, with deft ease, slipped from the ballgown. It settled at her feet in a wisp of satin and silk. He distantly noted her blushes were fewer, and she was more comfortable with her nakedness. Agatha removed her chemisette, baring her naked body to his gaze.

Hunger, sharp and insistent, tore through Thomas. She removed the blonde wig and tossed it aside. How provocative she appeared, yet her hair caught up in a chignon gave her a demure, ladylike grace. Pearls encircled her throat, and the softest blush pinkened her cheeks.

Below her neck ... her breasts were high and firm, the nipples lush and round like berries, the smoothness of her belly flat, and the arch of her hips flared enticingly. Her stockings stopped at mid-thigh and were held up by delicate silk garters. They made her legs seem long and supple. He lowered his gaze to the delicate dancing sippers that encased her feet.

Temptation dug sharply into his gut, and a warning whispered through him that he would barely survive this lesson.

"I am the tutor," he said, "not the student. How dare you think to give me a lesson?"

Those sweet lips curved, and she sauntered closer, slipping her hands slowly over his chest and up his nape.

"The auction is approaching faster than I

expected. I would hate to see the naked male body and faint from the sheer excitement of it."

"You teasing, minx."

She laughed, her eyes gleaming.

A very peculiar yet tender wisp of sensation rushed through Thomas. "So, you want me at your mercy."

"Never say you are afraid," she drawled.

He ruthlessly disciplined all the fire of lust and strange emotions twisting inside him. "I am yours to practice on as you please."

"I may be as wicked as I like?"

"I'm curious to see just how much you know about wickedness."

To keep his sanity, he resolved to remain firmly in his role as her tutor, no matter the temptation. She slipped her arm around his neck and pressed the side of her breast against his body.

"Too stiff, your body needs to be more pliant ... more sensual yet natural. Again."

Agatha swayed against him, sliding her hand up his chest and peeking at him from beneath her incredibly long lashes. "Like this?"

Thomas cleared his throat. "Better." *God, perfect ... you are perfect.*

A radiant smile lit her face, and she moved back. He tightened his arms around her and held her, just for a moment. Something in him was desperately hungry for the feel of her body against his.

"I would like to practice a few of the ... possible positions. I do not wish to appear gauche or startled when something is suggested. Bea and Ellen told me many men prefer it when women are on top *riding* or when we are on our knees with hips arched. I recall you mentioned this riding. I want to practice it."

"Very well."

She flicked the tip of her fingers across his chin. "Are there any lessons you would like to teach me tonight? In addition to the one I suggested?"

Deviltry gleamed in her gaze, and he suspected Agatha had another lesson in mind but was leading him to it, a regular rule in the game of coquetry that women employed. He arched a brow, and she licked along her bottom lip.

Ah ... *that* lesson.

Thomas obliged. He placed a thumb against her lower lip, exerting the slightest pressure until her lips parted. "I am going to teach you how to suck a cock."

"Do men like that?"

"Yes."

"Do you like it?"

Thomas was tempted to say his wants were irrelevant. "Yes."

"Then teach me," she whispered. "To use my tongue and lips and push a man toward release. But first ... teach me how to ride."

Bloody hell. He took a deep breath, stepped away from her and walked over to the large armchair. Thomas sat, his cock hardening even more. Her eyes widened, and she stared at his length before dragging her gaze up.

"Every man is different. Some smaller, some larger, some the same size."

"I see. Thank you for telling me."

He almost chuckled at that bit of politeness. "Come here."

She sauntered over, that delightful pink blushing over her body.

"Sit astride me."

"Like this?" she murmured, sitting in his lap, her legs caging his knees.

His belly rippled, and he clenched his teeth. He moved a little, adjusting his position so that the hard ridge of his cock nestled against her mound. The feel of his stalk against her bare pussy was already torture. Perhaps he should put on his trousers for this lesson.

"You can face me ... or give me your back, but your legs should bracket each of my thighs."

"Oh," she said, grabbing the headrest. "I

would prefer to face you. Your eyes are so beautiful, Thomas. I always feel like I'm being pulled under when I hold your gaze."

Their eyes met, and his heartbeat quickened. "Are you practicing the art of flattery now?"

"A man likes his vanity stroked," she purred, her tone laced with playful confidence. "Did I delight yours?"

He smiled. *Yes.* "You can place your hands on my shoulders to balance your weight or slip them around my nape. Your lover can either place his hands on your hips or hug them around your back, or thrust his fingers into your hair and arch your throat."

Agatha nodded and slipped her hands up to clasp his shoulders. Thomas wanted to get a dagger and stabbed himself in the heart. How stupid to have suggested she could pretend to ride him to learn the rhythm. He was a glutton for torture.

"Like that," he hissed through gritted teeth.

His cock throbbed, and she looked down.

A soft shudder went through her body. "Usually, ... your cock would be inside my body."

"Yes. We'll pretend."

"Have you ever done that before?"

"Done what?"

Her gaze lingered on his face, a faint smile on her lips. "Imagined yourself ... inside me."

227

"That knowledge is hardly relevant to your lesson," he replied.

Her rich and unguarded laugh struck him like a spark, intensifying his awareness of her warmth and allure.

"When you're on his cock, you'll want to move—slowly at first, then up and down, finding a rhythm," he instructed, keeping his tone steady. "While I am not in you, you can still practice the motion."

She released one of his shoulders to unpin her hair, letting it drop in a silken waterfall. Agatha surprised him by coasting that hand up his chest to cup his jaw and hold his gaze.

"Your eyes are truly beautiful," she said softly.

Then she undulated. It was fucking laughable the way his cock jerked and his balls burned as if he was already close to a climax. She moved up and down, her body awkward.

"Slower ... feel your weight, find your balance, and get comfortable before you pick up the pace."

Agatha wrinkled her nose. "Perhaps I should learn to ride the horse first. However, I do not think that is logical. I have never seen a man or a woman bouncing atop their horse when they ride, and Bea said it was like bouncing."

She sounded irritated, and he scowled,

wondering if he was the only one losing his damn mind. Agatha reached between them and clasped his cock.

Sweet mercy. "Agatha—"

"My fingers can barely meet around your ... manroot."

A choking sound left him, and she laughed, her lovely eyes gleaming.

"I thought it sounded ridiculous, too. Did you know some women called it plug-tail?"

Thomas could not answer, for the damn woman tightened her fingers around his cock, and rubbed the flared, mushroomed head along her slit.

"Oh," she gasped. "It feels ... *good*."

He tensed, gripping her hips with such strength she would likely have a bruise. He forced his fingers to relax when she did it again.

"Can I do this and not allow ... this inside?"

"No."

"Why not?" she bit her lips, her eyes half-closed as she rubbed the tip of his cock against her slit.

"It would not be enough," he hissed, his balls tightening.

"Does it feel good to you, too?"

"Yes."

"But you need more?"

"Yes, because more feels better."

"I cannot imagine it," she gasped, arching her hips.

He stroked down her back, trailing his fingers along her spine. It took all his self-control not to grip her hips tighter and drag her pussy onto his length. Over and over, she tormented him until she found her rhythm and started to undulate against him. His cock flexed against her flesh, the head ruddy and flushed. There were times the soft opening of her cunt caught on the edge of his cock, and she would whimper, glide upward and return down.

Bloody hell.

This lesson would kill him.

❦

NEITHER BEA nor Ellen had explained that sensual torture was double-edged. The ache inside her sex was sharp and insistent, peaking with each glide of her folds over his shaft. Thomas touched Agatha everywhere. Her breasts were so sensitive that each stroke of his fingers over her nipples caused a helpless moan to slip from her. He looked at her with pure male appreciation and hunger. She looked down and watched as he caressed her throbbing tips to straining redness. "This is too distracting," she whispered.

"The man who takes you might not leave all the control to you. It is also a pleasure for him to learn your body, even if for his own selfish satisfaction. His hands will not be idle; do you understand?"

"Yes." She was already desperately wet, for her body knew the pleasure his touch could inflict.

She rolled her hips, sliding her sex over the smooth hardness of his cock. He groaned, sank his fingers deeper into the armrest, and arched his throat. His gaze narrowed, and a hiss escaped him when she rolled her hips again and moved as if slowly riding, incorporating the lessons learned in the eastern dance.

Each rub of her folds over his hard length spiked her arousal, and she became wetter. Agatha drew a deep, shuddering breath, fighting for control. There was an aching, empty sensation low in her belly. She understood enough about coupling to know that she might find fulfillment once he was inside her body. She bit her bottom lip when his thickness slipped along her folds and pressed insistently at her entrance. Agatha bore down a little, desperate to be filled but careful not to be too exuberant.

He groaned, and she whimpered at the tight, stretching sensation before rolling her hips and unrooting him from the position. Over and over, she teased him, slicking her flesh over his cock, back and forth, up and down. A low, almost burning pressure in her belly was desperate for release.

"Agatha ... *fuck* ..."

Carnal power rolled through her, and she leaned into her roll, brushing her lips against his. Thomas's arms closed around her back, and his mouth covered hers, hard and voracious. One of his hands slid through her hair, gripping it as his tongue penetrated her mouth. Their tongues dueled with passionate demand, and he groaned deep in his throat, the sound vibrating in her own mouth. They kissed for several moments before he released her with a harsh sound. Her lips felt bruised, yet the sensations throbbing low in her belly were not fright but of alarming want.

"You are so wet," he groaned.

A sensual smile crossed his lips as he watched her through lowered lids. Yet his jaw was clenched. Agatha realized he was exerting an enormous will not to ravish her. She couldn't decide if she should be frightened or thrilled.

He gripped her hips to hold her in place, delved his hand between their bodies and speared two fingers inside her sex.

"Thomas!" Agatha couldn't contain the cry of pleasure that swelled in her chest.

"Ride my fingers," he said, his voice a dark throb of lust.

Feeling him there assuaging the emptiness urged her to glide up and down instead of the slow, teasing roll. His fingers remained buried deep in her quivering pussy while his thumb rubbed her clitoris. Far sooner than she anticipated, delirious pleasure swept through Agatha as she shattered, and she rode the sweet wave of ecstasy, trembling and moaning.

His fingers slipped from her and lightly teased her belly. "How is my ride, my lord?" she murmured, rolling back her hips in a teasing swivel.

He thrust his fingers through her hair and tugged her mouth close. "I am so tempted to fuck you right here."

"You can."

His gaze narrowed to a slit, and he froze. "What did you say?"

Though his manhood size and intensity intimated her, she drawled, "Five thousand pounds, and I am yours for the night. There would be no need for an auction."

"No."

Agatha kissed his chin. "I thought you would say that."

A pang of disappointment went through her heart, and she shimmied off his body and lowered herself to her knees onto the lush carpet. He rose, his cock heavy and engorged as he reached for her. She slid her hands up his thighs, and he froze. She looked up at him, letting him see the unguarded hunger unfurling within her, solely for him.

CHAPTER 19

Thomas gazed down at Agatha, his breath hitching as her delicate hands encircled his throbbing erection. She leaned in, her breath a silken, heated caress against his flesh. His gut clenched, and he swallowed hard, fighting to maintain control. Agatha began tentatively, her tongue tracing a slow, sensual glide along his cock, eliciting a groan from Thomas. He savored the wet heat of her mouth, the sensation sending hot shards of pleasure coursing through his body.

One of her hands fluttered to his hips, exploring the contours of his muscles. God, he never knew a touch as curious and innocent as this could make him this hungry for more. Thomas inhaled deeply, restraining his mounting need, determined to give her all the time she needed to indulge in this newfound intimacy. He watched as heated sensuality darkened her eyes.

Her lips trailed down the rigid length, and his balls ached, a sharp, almost unbearable pleasure as her wet tongue caressed them. Lust shivered through him, tingling up to the tip of his cock, flexing it with a desperate need. Agatha made a low sound of pleasure, then her swollen lips parted to cover the engorged, sensitive head of his cock. Thomas groaned, his control slipping further with each teasing flick of her tongue.

Her hair cascaded over her face, obscuring his view, and he gripped it, wrapping it around his hand, guiding her movements. Watching her suck his cock into her untried mouth was hotter and more intense than anything he could have imagined. The sight of her, so eager and uninhibited, filled him with lust so intense he felt intoxicated.

"Good," he praised, his voice rough with restraint, remembering he should teach her to improve.

A knife-like pain cut from his chest down to his gut, a specter that rose inside him whenever he thought of another man touching her. He ruthlessly cut it away, focusing on the present, on the raw, unfiltered pleasure.

"Suck a little tighter ... good ... easy ... that choking feel is natural ... go slower ... go—"

His words got lost in a groan as she curled her tongue and then sucked with a stronger pull, her mouth a vice of pleasure around him.

"Who taught you that?" The words hissed from him before he could control the savage feeling tearing through his chest.

She fucking winked, her brilliant green eyes daring him to react. Narrowing his gaze, Thomas tightened his grip on her hair and slowly pulled his length from a bliss that felt unknown.

"Who taught you?" he demanded, the cold warning in his tone unmistakable.

"Jealous?" she purred.

Her eyes were drowsy, heavy-lidded, but she stared at him with that wicked gleam of challenge, daring him to do something ... but what?

Thomas stilled, his frown deepening. *Jealousy?* He had lived, laughed, and known hurt, fury, joy, and annoyance for years, but jealousy was an emotion he had never encountered.

Bloody hell.

Agatha raked her teeth over his cock head, and he moaned, a sound he had never made for a lover. Thomas tightened his hand in her hair and slowly worked his cock inside her sweet hot mouth with firm, shallow strokes. It was sheer torture and paradise.

He encircled her throat with his other hand, holding her close and sliding his cock as deep down her throat as it would go. She made a muffled sound around his length, and her eyes watered, but he continued fucking her mouth with slow ease. He was lost in the scorching heat of her mouth, overwhelmed by the raw carnality she unleashed and the innocent hunger with which she claimed him. Agatha shifted, closing her thighs together.

"Open them."

Her cheeks flushed, and she eased her knees open on the carpet.

"That ache you are feeling will not leave. Rub your fingers on your clitoris."

Another moan around his cock, before she slipped her hands low over her belly, sliding them through her soaked pussy. She looked exquisitely provocative: her jaw hollowed, lips parted as she drew him deeper, cheeks flushed with the fervor of desire. Her eyes, dark with arousal, glittered and her hair spilled in wild, untamed waves around her shoulders. Her skin glistened with a sheen of sweat that accentuated every lush curve, each hollow and rise of her body. The delicate garters clung to her thighs, somehow innocent yet seductive, while her dancing shoes remained, a final touch of demureness in wicked, erotic contrast to her intoxicating abandon.

Seeing Agatha like this would be etched into his memory; years from now, he knew he would still recall this moment. In the past, once he moved on from a lover, he never allowed them to linger in his thoughts. But Agatha was different, slipping past his defenses and leaving an indelible mark.

"Work your pussy faster," he commanded. "Use three fingers and press harder against your clitoris with each glide."

She shuddered and climaxed; her gaze widened with stunned disbelief.

Ah, my sweet, you are still so beautifully innocent. And by God, I want to unravel and debauch you.

❧

THOMAS PULLED AWAY FROM AGATHA, his teeth gritted as he fought to regain control. A thrill of satisfaction and delight coursed through her, realizing she'd unraveled his cool, unshakable control to this point. He grabbed his cock, his fingers wrapping around the thick, throbbing shaft, and tilted his head back, his eyes closed as he tried to remaster himself.

"You did not attain pleasure like I did,"

Agatha said, her voice husky, reaching out to glide her finger across his smooth crown.

Thomas's throat worked on a tight swallow, and he stepped back. "It is not necessary," he said, his voice strained.

Agatha performed a happy dance in her thoughts before delicately clearing her throat. "Why?" she pressed, her eyes never leaving his face, searching for answers in the carnal lines of his expression.

"The best way to master oneself is through denial or ..."

"Or you might do more than you want," she said softly, "like *thoroughly* ravish me."

"Yes," he said, his grip tightening around his cock.

I want you, too, she silently cried, her heart aching. "I want to see your release. What is it like?"

Thomas lifted a brow.

"You have seen my release, and I have not seen yours. You've mentioned that men and women self-pleasure. Show me."

His mouth quirked, and he moved to the chaise, sprawling on it like an emperor, his body a study in raw, primal beauty. Agatha's breath caught in her throat as she watched him. He clasped his thick stalk, his hand moving with a practiced rhythm, his eyes half-closed as he held her stare.

Agatha's heart pounded. She had never seen anything so beautiful, and the sight of him, so unguarded, pierced her chest with that sweet, almost frightening emotion. His face was a harsh but sensual grimace of lust.

"Thomas," she softly said, "You look ... magnificent."

Agatha could feel the heat of his desire, the raw, unbridled passion that seemed to pulse through the room, drawing her in, making her want to reach out and touch him, to feel the heat of his skin against hers. Still on her knees, she glided forward, her gaze locked on his. With a flicker of her tongue, she traced over the sensitive, flared head of his cock, watching his reaction. Thomas groaned, his head falling back as he continued to stroke himself, his body arching.

"Do it again," he murmured, his voice thick with desire.

This time she sucked, raking her teeth on the underside before releasing him from her lips.

"*Fuck!*"

He jerked his hands twice, and he reached his climax with his body tense and muscles straining. Thomas's low, guttural sound of pleasure skated over her skin, igniting a heat deep in her belly that pulsed with a fierce, undeniable desire.

Agatha rose and crossed to the mantle, pouring whisky into two glasses. She handed him one, then settled at the opposite end of the chaise, acutely aware of her nakedness and that she wore only stockings, garters, and dancing slippers. She enjoyed the appreciative gleam in his gaze, even as a faint blush warmed her skin. Curling one leg beneath her, she brought the glass to her lips, savoring a sip.

"Thomas."

His gaze collided with hers. "Hmm?"

"Ellen ... she mentioned that she had a lover who took pleasure in ... her arse. From her experience, I presumed she couldn't be mistaken. She implied that many gentlemen at *Aphrodite* look for a lover willing to ..."

His eyes glinted with humor. "Yes. Your winner might desire to take you there."

Her heart skipped a beat; the idea still left her breathless. "Will it hurt?"

"Yes."

Startled, her eyes widened. "Is it also painful for the man?"

A deceptively sensual smile curved mouth. "No. But if he plays with your pussy, especially your clitoris, the pleasure can blend with the pain until they're indistinguishable."

"And … if he doesn't?" she asked, fighting to keep her voice steady.

"Then you'll bear the pain, and walking may be challenging for a few days."

Goodness. "Would you … want that?"

A flicker of heat flashed in his gaze before he reined it in. "This isn't about me, Agatha. I already told you I won't be bidding."

That heavy sensation once again pressed against her chest. "Are you certain you would not bid for me?"

His mouth lifted in a half-smile. "Yes."

Agatha lowered her lashes for a moment, hoping to hide her disappointment. "Can I set this as a boundary?"

"Anything can be forbidden."

"But … once again, making myself unavailable in that manner will deter some, won't it? Considering Ellen's words, it seemed all the men at *Aphrodite* … like that."

"Yes. If they know even your arse is also untouched, it might drive the bidding higher," he replied, his voice a husky drawl, eyes gleaming with an almost dangerous sensuality.

Awareness forcibly struck her heart. "You like it, don't you? Taking a woman there …"

"It has its appeal."

"Show me," she murmured, sensing he enjoyed it more than he was letting on.

The glass lifting to his mouth froze. "What?"

She smirked, sensing she'd unsettled him. "I want you to use your fingers ... let me experience it, just enough to understand. Once without teasing of my sex ... and once with your touch on my clitoris. That way, I can decide whether it should be a boundary."

"Lie on your belly on the chaise by the fire," he murmured.

A tremor of nerves fluttered through her, but she rose from the sofa, steadying herself as she crossed the room. Agatha lay on her stomach across the plush, oversized chaise, feeling the luxurious softness cradling her body. The rich scent of lavender mingled with the earthy notes of Thomas's rousing scent calmed and heightened her senses.

Agatha closed her eyes, breathing steadily. He positioned a cushion beneath her hips, creating a soft arch. She sank deeper into the anticipation of his touch.

Thomas's warm and strong hands settled on her shoulders. The first press of his thumbs into her tense muscles made her exhale, and her body relaxed under the glide of his fingers.

She had not anticipated this. The lavender oil slicked her skin, making every movement fluid, his fingers kneading away any remnants of her tension. Agatha moaned, acutely aware of everything—the roughness of his palms against the softness of her skin, the way his breath fanned lightly against her neck, and the undeniable heat that radiated from his body so close to hers.

"Is this always a precursor to ... arse play?" she murmured, her voice tinged with nerves and a hint of teasing.

Thomas's low chuckle rippled over her senses, deep and intimate.

"No," he said. "This is simply because you've been working hard. Madam Rebecca mentioned you've been practicing dancing for hours each day."

A warmth spread through her chest, unexpected and achingly sweet. "It feels ... glorious. Thank you."

"There are no thanks needed between friends." His hand trailed down her spine, igniting every inch of her skin he touched. "Did I not mention this before?"

She turned her head slightly, attempting to hide her smile. "Are you finally accepting that we're friends?"

"Hmm." He paused as if mulling over the word, his fingers brushing in light circles against her lower back. "A novelty for me, but I like you, Agatha."

Her heart stuttered, his words settling

deeper than she'd anticipated. She lowered her gaze, whispering, "I like you, too."

He worked his way down her back in slow, unhurried strokes, his hands skilled in coaxing out any resistance. Every touch evoked a surge of warmth that blossomed low in her belly. His strong and confident hands skimmed over her thighs, tracing their outer curves, lingering as if memorizing her. When he reached the curve of her lower back, his palms smoothed over her hips, and a thrill sparked through her.

Agatha's fingers clenched slightly against the cushion as he moved to massage her buttocks, his touch firm yet somehow reverent. He lowered his head, his breath hot against her skin, and bit gently into the swell of one buttock cheek. The sensation sent a jolt of pleasure through her, and a low groan escaped her lips before she could suppress it. Her skin tingled, every nerve alive under his mouth and hands.

"Do you enjoy this?"

Her answer came as a soft hum, an involuntary arch of her back pressing her closer to his touch. The feel of him so close was intoxicating. Every brush of his fingers, every press of his palm, seemed to reach inside her, leaving her senses heightened, raw, and wanting.

Thomas's oiled fingers brushed her shoulders, gliding smoothly down her back with gentle, deliberate pressure, tracing the curve of her spine. She could feel every precise touch, each stroke heightening her awareness of him. Agatha wasn't just aware of him—she was consumed.

"Are you ready?" His voice was a low murmur, gentle and reassuring, wrapping around her like warmth itself.

Agatha nodded, her pulse racing, excitement and curiosity threading through her. She trusted him with her body. When his fingers reached the cleft of her derriere, he pressed his lips to her shoulder, his kiss lingering, soft and slow. Agatha's breath hitched, and her belly tightened. A single oiled finger slid into her arse, and she gasped at the sting.

"Relax," he murmured, his voice a soothing balm. "Let yourself feel every moment."

He moved his finger, working it deeper until she melted beneath his touch. Just as her breath steadied, he leaned forward, his mouth brushing over her lower back, his teeth grazing the globe of her arse, gentle but possessive.

Soon, another finger joined the first, and a gasp escaped her, sharp and unbidden, fire searing her back entrance. "Thomas," she cried, gripping the cushion. "It hurts."

"I know."

A whimper escaped her when he started to

work his fingers deeper, stretching those unused muscles.

"My cock is much thicker than these two fingers," he said. "A considerate lover will prepare and liberally oil you to take him. It will still hurt."

His voice was a low murmur, rich with carnality and something darker. Thomas's thrust was steady and deep, and she couldn't help the sob that whispered from her. Perspiration beaded on her shoulders and trickled over her neck, between her breasts.

"Thomas?"

"Reach under your body and play with your pussy for me."

Agatha arched slightly, the move impaling his fingers deeper. She slipped her hand between the tight fit of her body and the chaise, desperately reaching for her sex. She rubbed her fingers over her clitoris, and it felt as if lightning struck her.

Oh!

"Good?" he whispered, his voice thick and slightly husky.

She turned her head to look at him, her face flushed, eyes heavy with arousal. "Yes ... so good," she breathed, her voice a tremor of pleasure and need, eagerly reaching for the sparks of pleasure now cracking through her body, drowning out the pain in her rear.

Agatha felt herself arching, wordlessly asking for more. A smile played at the corner of his lips as his fingers pressed deeper and more firmly. Agatha surrendered to the erotic pleasure-pain, her heart pounding as he explored her in ways that unraveled her completely. Her fingers worked her clitoris in time with his strokes until she writhed with the need to release.

"*Thomas!*" she screamed his name into the cushion when he slipped in a third finger.

She pressed down hard on her nub, and heat bloomed through her body, the flood of ecstasy so intense it bordered on pain. Agatha's body turned pliant, and she turned her head to weakly look at him. His manhood was once again hard, but Thomas ignored his arousal, gently removed his fingers and walked toward the bath chamber. She closed her eyes, exhaustion pulling her under. Something cool touched her flesh, and she opened her eyes.

He used a wet washcloth to clean her body gently. A lump formed in her throat as she stared at him. He finished cleaning her and went to his bath chamber for a few minutes before returning. Thomas lay down behind her and curved her into his side. She was left breathless when he pulled her closer, his mouth capturing hers in a lingering kiss.

This is not a lesson ...

The temptation to curl into his chest was almost overpowering. He would hold her, and she could sleep warmly and safely in his arms. She had never felt that way with anyone before. Thomas had the potential to make her want the things she'd convinced herself she could live without. This man made her feel with such intensity that Agatha never dreamed was possible.

The realization was terrifying.

She had never fallen in love, but that did not diminish her conviction that she was tumbling headlong into love with Thomas.

CHAPTER 20

Still innocent.

Thomas saw it in the soft, luminous stare and dazed look in her eyes. Agatha smiled, yawned and snuggled into his embrace. It struck him rather forcibly that a lover had never lingered within his arms. He frowned, peering down at her. Agatha's mere existence cracked open something unknown inside Thomas. Hell, he had once thought of himself in love and had offered marriage. That feeling was sweet and hopeful. Whatever this was with Agatha, it felt like a fucking obsession. Another unknown sensation crept inside his chest, and he pressed his mouth against her forehead, slamming his eyes closed.

Her touch, so delicate, uncertain even, yet so seductive, drifted over his chest. "Your heartbeat is increasing."

Thomas buried his face in the curve of her shoulder, breathing her in, savoring the softness of her skin and the sweetness of her scent. His arousal was nearly unbearable, the intensity frustrating. Every part of him ached to taste her, to lose himself in her completely. He wanted to slide his tongue over her delicate folds until she shattered, then take her—slow and deep, his need overwhelming. He had never wanted a woman so fiercely, and resisting was challenging.

The thought struck him: she would no longer need the auction if he gave in and made her his. Perhaps he could make her an offer that would keep her by his side. Yet hell, he'd never kept a mistress. He'd enjoyed lovers, paid his membership fees to *Aphrodite*, and had given gifts to a few ladies he visited, but never had he considered a lasting arrangement with a woman. Such a liaison would require trust and intimacy he guarded fiercely, boundaries he had no intention of allowing anyone to cross.

"Do you think I am ready for the auction?"

Her soft question surprised him; he thought she had drifted off to sleep.

"I do not know," he admitted. "Tupping ... lovemaking ... fucking ... intimacy—they're vast worlds in themselves. Even if we had a year, I doubt I could teach you everything I know. And your bidder may be even more knowledgeable than I am."

She traced a finger over his chest, a light, tantalizing movement that sent ripples over his skin.

"You said that men have fantasies they wish to see fulfilled. That's why they're members of *Aphrodite*."

"Yes."

She leaned back, lifting her face to his. "I am very curious about the fantasies that torment you."

He stilled, caught off guard. "I have never denied myself anything I want. There is no longing left unfulfilled." Yet, the words that usually rang so true now felt hollow.

Her lips curved. "You live a life of excess. Is that why they call you a rake and a scoundrel?"

Thomas wondered how much Bea and Ellen discussed with Agatha. "I live a life of pleasure and contentment."

She wrinkled her nose with a bemused smile. "It is astonishing that a life could exist where every desire is met."

He brushed his knuckles along the bridge of her nose. "What have you longed for, Agatha?"

She laughed softly. "I do not dare long for anything beyond what I can achieve. Risk is ...

dangerous. I never thought of myself as a lady who indulges in risky pursuits."

"Taking risks brings its own rewards."

She raised an elegant brow. "Even the dangerous ones?"

"Especially those."

"I suppose I am taking a risk auctioning myself, but it feels more like a business decision, something sensible. The outcome is beneficial; the cost ... I can measure. But the rewards are certain."

A wistful tone crept into her voice, and something in her eyes softened.

"What are you thinking of right now?"

She hesitated, and then a rueful smile touched her mouth. "I was remembering a conversation I had with my mother the year she died. I told her I wanted a husband like my papa and at least six children. He'd sing to her as she baked, pulling her to dance around the kitchen. She'd laugh and wave him off, but later, she'd find him just to hug him. I thought happiness was as simple as marriage and children. When I told my mother, she kissed me and said I'd find a man who'd adore me, just as Papa loved her."

A harsh ache settled in his chest. "You no longer want this?"

"I haven't dreamed of such things in years. What would be the point of it now? Such whimsy is for ladies who have the luxury of support."

"You are beautiful. Surely, many men have tried to win your favor."

She laughed, the sound rippling through him, leaving a peculiar warmth in its wake.

"A few did, but none seemed interested in knowing who I was. There was a man ... before I moved to Devonshire. He asked me to marry him, and I said yes."

The unexpected jealousy that clawed at him almost had him scowling.

"When I came to *Aphrodite* last year, I knew I'd have to explain I was forced to settle my father's debt. I knew he'd never marry me after. My stepmother urged me to keep silent; she knew he had a lover and cautioned that my lack of chastity was not something for him to consider. However, I couldn't do it. It felt dishonest and wrong. Luckily, the Duke of Basil was there that night, and he saved me from having to sell myself."

Thomas jerked, shock rippling through him. "Basil saved you?"

Her eyes gleamed with amusement. "You seem so surprised."

He laughed, rubbing a hand over his face. "Basil is one of my closest friends."

Agatha's eyes widened. "Can the world be so small?"

"No," he said dryly, "but *Aphrodite* is. Friends of similar inclinations flock together. We met as lads, went to the same university, and indulged in the same debauchery."

She studied him, her gaze tender as her fingers traced the corner of his mouth. "Kindness and compassion bind you two as much as your ... pleasures."

"I am not—"

"Yes, you are not kind," she interrupted, smiling warmly. "So you keep saying."

Bloody hell. Thomas felt he did not know how to form coherent thoughts when she looked at him like that. "Would you like to join me at the theatre tomorrow?"

Delight sparked in her eyes. "The Theatre Royal in Covent Gardens?"

"Yes."

"I have heard it is magnificent." She yawned, then stifled a laugh against his chest. "Will Ronald be there?"

"I hadn't planned to ask him. Sometimes he abhors crowds."

"Please tell him a beautiful lady wishes for a handsome man to escort her to the theatre."

He grunted. "And what am I?"

"Our brave guard, there to protect us from whispers and prying eyes."

Thomas smiled, wondering how a woman so different from anyone he'd ever met could feel so unexpectedly familiar.

"Ronald is still in Bath with my mother, sister, and aunt," Thomas said. "My mother plans to return at the end of the season. However, I'll write to him and mention that you're longing to enjoy an evening graced by his handsomeness."

She laughed, a soft sound that burrowed into his chest, and she nestled closer as if wanting to melt into him.

"Do you think about your father?"

Hell. The question slipped out before he'd even processed it.

"Sometimes," she replied quietly. "But I don't long for him."

"What will you do after ... the auction?"

"Return home to my family," she answered without hesitation. "I miss them terribly, and they'll be relieved I'm back. I want to plan carefully and save every bit for their futures. Maggie dreams of becoming a renowned modiste. Sarah and Carson ... well, they haven't begun dreaming yet. Gloria has always wanted a bakery, and Henry adores horses. I think he'd make an excellent stable master, so I'll try to find him an apprenticeship."

That familiar pang twisted in his chest, sharper than before. "And what plans do you have for yourself?"

A wistful smile touched her lips. "Providing for my family is for myself as much as it is for them."

By God, she was selfless to her very bones. Yet he understood, all too well, that fierce loyalty and sense of duty. Thomas wanted to know her better—what foods she enjoyed, what books delighted her, and if she slept sprawled or curled up. He wanted to undress her, spend hours entwined with her, and then take her to the opera, balls, on long walks, exploring the open sea on his yacht. He wanted her laughter, her warmth, her everything. But only for a moment.

"Did you love your fiancée?"

Bloody hell. "I do not know," he replied after a pause.

"Is that possible, not to know?"

"I was ... young," he said. "At the time, I wasn't indifferent to the idea of marriage and was even eager to find my countess, which delighted my mother. I enjoyed Lady Eva's company and the dances we shared."

"How do you feel when you see her now?"

Thomas frowned. "I'm not certain I have. If I have, I looked past her without realizing it. I cut her from my thoughts completely."

Agatha pressed her hands against his chest, leaning closer to search his gaze. "You simply excised her from your awareness?"

"Yes."

She reached up and traced a finger along the scar on his cheek. "How ... how did you get this scar?"

A humorless smile touched his lips. "I fought a duel."

Her eyes widened. "Why?"

"We anticipated our vows," he said with dry amusement.

"Is that your delicate way of saying you tupped her before marriage?"

Thomas chuckled. "Yes. When I ended the engagement, her brother threatened a suit and then challenged me to a duel. I suspect she shared just how ... intimate we were."

"And you still wouldn't marry her?"

"No."

"That is ... rather ruthless," she murmured.

"Those who harm my loved ones are not forgiven. They taunted and tormented my brother at her urging, and she found it entertaining. That woman would never be a part of my family."

Her eyes softened, a glimmer of understanding there that struck him. "What happened in the duel?"

"I knew refusing would be dishonorable," he said, his tone edged with irony, "given that I knew what I was risking by having her in my bed before marriage. I accepted and won. But as I lowered my rapier, her brother lunged at me. It was a cheap attack, and he sliced my cheek."

"That wretch," she snapped, her gaze fierce. "What did you do to him?"

He lifted a brow. "I let him off. I told him that the loss of my beauty would settle the loss of his sister's chastity."

Agatha reached up and kissed the corner of his scar. "Only a vain scoundrel would believe this scratch could mar his handsomeness," she whispered, her lips lingering close to his.

Thomas wrapped his arms around her, kissing her mouth for endless moments. And as he closed his eyes and she placed her face on his chest, he couldn't bring himself to suggest she return to her own room.

THE CROWD outside the theatre buzzed with anticipation, a vibrant mix of laughter, chatter, and the occasional shout from vendors hawking their wares. Agatha, dressed in a stunning rose-colored gown, glanced about, her excitement palpable. She looked radiant, her hair swept elegantly into a chignon, with delicate tendrils framing her face and catching the soft glow of the gas lamps. Her gaze sparkled as it drifted over London's finest, who milled around the entrance in exquisite attire, the air alive with sophistication and spectacle.

Just ahead, Thomas noticed a familiar face in the crowd. "Basil," he murmured, steering Agatha towards the Duke of Basil and his wife Elizabeth.

The duke spotted Thomas, his eyes lighting up in recognition.

"Radbourne," he greeted. "I have not seen you at the theatre in ages."

The duke's gaze shifted to Agatha, a hint of surprise flickering before a look of recognition softened his expression. "And you, my lady. I believe we've met before."

Agatha's face softened. "Indeed, Your Grace," she replied, lowering into a curtsy. "I cannot thank you enough for last year ... your kindness to my family has not been forgotten."

Basil inclined his head. "Allow me to introduce you to Elizabeth, my duchess," he said, gesturing to his wife with a proud smile.

"Elizabeth, this is Miss Woodville, a ... friend of Radbourne."

The duchess extended her hand with warmth, her smile teasing as she looked toward Thomas. "A pleasure to meet you, Agatha. I've heard much of Lord Radbourne's elusive nature at social events, and I can see why he might make an exception this evening. My brother has mentioned Radbourne's fascination."

Agatha's wrinkled her nose. "Your brother mentioned it, Your Grace?"

Elizabeth's eyes gleamed with amusement. "Yes, Mr. Brandon Armstrong."

Agatha blinked, surprised. "*Oh*," she murmured, smiling. "You share the same beautiful smile and eyes."

"Ah, I am easily won by flattery," Elizabeth drawled, her smile widening. "Now, won't you join us in our box? Please call me Bette!"

Agatha hesitated for a moment. "You do know I am from *Aphrodite*?"

Basil let out a chuckle. "Not everyone in the *ton* is inclined to sit with a stick up their arse."

Elizabeth gasped, swatting him lightly, and Agatha laughed, pressing her gloved hand to her mouth to muffle the sound.

"It would be our honor to have you with us," Elizabeth insisted, her warmth unwavering.

"Thank you." Agatha flushed and glanced at

Thomas, her emerald gaze gleaming with pleasure.

They ascended the grand staircase and entered the opulent interior.

"It is magnificent," Agatha said.

The theatre was indeed breathtaking, almost palatial in its grandeur. Gilded chandeliers cast a warm glow over the crimson velvet seats and curtains, the drapes tied back with luxurious gold tassels. Marble columns supported a soaring ceiling painted with scenes of myth and legend, where cherubs seemed to float dreamily across a field of stars. The faint strains of the orchestra tuning their instruments floated in the air, mingling with the scent of polished wood and perfume.

As they entered the duke's private box, Agatha gasped softly. The box was a sanctuary of elegance, draped in rich crimson fabric, with plush seating that afforded a perfect view of the stage. Below them, the audience filled in, a swirl of gentry and socialites glittering under the chandeliers.

Whispers trailed after them, fans snapped open to hide curious glances, and lorgnettes discreetly focused on Agatha and Thomas.

"Why is everyone staring?" Agatha asked quietly, turning to Thomas.

Thomas's gaze lingered on her. "Because you

are the most beautiful woman here. They cannot look away."

Elizabeth leaned over with a mischievous grin. "It's true, Agatha. But they are just as intrigued by Radbourne's presence here with you. The *ton* is not used to him being so ... visible in society. They are more than curious."

Just then, a whisper reached their ears from a nearby box.

"Isn't that the lady he danced with at Lady Rafferty's ball? The hair might appear different, but I could never forget such a face or that smile."

"She must be his mistress," came another murmur. "And this is the third time he's been seen with her in public."

Agatha's brows drew together, though a glimmer of humor shone in her eyes. "Why do they care who I am? What business is it of theirs?"

Elizabeth leaned closer with a knowing smile. "Ignore them. Mystery suits you beautifully."

Thomas remained unbothered by the attention, exchanging glances with Basil, who shared an amused smirk. A hush settled over the crowd as the orchestra struck its opening notes, the curtains sweeping back to reveal the stage. Agatha leaned forward, her eyes filled with wonder, captivated by the spectacle before her. Yet Thomas's gaze lingered on her, absorbing every flicker of excitement that crossed her face. He should have been watching the performance, but his lover commanded his attention.

She is not my lover, he reminded himself, the thought leaving a strange ache within him. But as he watched her, he couldn't shake the feeling that she was becoming more than a fleeting fascination. *What am I to do with you, Agatha?*

CHAPTER 21

A gatha lay awake, stretching languidly, a delicate yawn escaping her lips. Thomas had only just delivered her home after a midnight stroll in Hyde Park that had somehow stretched into hours. They'd climbed a tree together, laughing at the sheer silliness of their actions, perched on a sturdy branch, sharing stories. The nights had been enchanting, and the days were filled with sights and sounds she'd only imagined in far-off dreams, and a part of her dearly wished it would never end.

Exhausted yet exhilarated, she found herself returning to *Aphrodite* at dawn each day, glowing from the adventures she'd shared with Thomas around town. Just last night, they strolled the sprawling pathways of Vauxhall Gardens. They watched acrobats swing with breathtaking precision across the tightropes, and men balanced on horseback, performing daring feats that had her gasping. The night sky erupted in a cascade of fireworks, casting radiant colors that mirrored the flutter of excitement in her chest. Beside her, Thomas seemed at ease, the sharp edges of his usual reserve softened as he watched her.

This had bemused Agatha. He didn't seem to find Vauxhall Gardens as diverting and delightful as she did, instead watching her reactions intently as though he could only feel pleasure through hers. The night before, he'd taken her to yet another society ball, and she danced the waltz with him twice. Many guests' gazes lingered on her with curiosity and envy. Agatha noticed the whispers intensifying each time she was seen on Thomas's arm and the curious stares and raised brows as people tried to piece together her story.

How appalled they would be if they knew the truth—that her hands had once milked cows, scrubbed pots, and carried baskets of freshly baked bread through town. Agatha and Thomas had also shared a picnic at Hampstead Heath, where the fresh scent of earth and grass mingled with the sweet taste of fresh strawberries and honey cakes. The Royal Museum tour captivated her as she gawked at marble statues and ancient relics, absorbing the knowledge Thomas shared. She felt a pang in her chest, realizing how naturally she could fit into this world if it weren't for her circumstances.

Even Bea had joined in her amusement, rushing to her chamber yesterday to gleefully present the latest scandal sheet. It hinted that Agatha must be of some noble birth or even royalty, connected as she was to a duke, a marquess, and an earl, though her identity remained shrouded in mystery. Agatha had laughed at the notion, finding it comical that society could elevate her status so easily based on appearances alone, while they'd likely recoil in horror at her true origins.

Yet amid the laughter and delight, a heavy ache settled in her heart. She longed for this life —to live within Thomas's world. Some of her felt she could belong there, yet she knew it was impossible. It was evident Thomas only saw her as a momentary spark in his otherwise jaded existence. She would eventually fade into the background in his life of luxury and privilege, a novelty that wore thin once her allure was unraveled.

Though their private lessons were wickedly intimate, and he seemed captivated by her responses, his restraint outside those moments told her far more than words ever could. She was only a diversion to a man of his experience.

Agatha fought the longing that surged within her. She couldn't afford to let herself keep falling so deeply. She stifled another yawn, letting her eyes drift shut as sleep finally claimed her. A sharp knock startled Agatha, dragging her from the haze of restless sleep. Her heart leaped in her chest as she sat up, disoriented for a moment, until she heard Bea's voice through the door.

"Agatha, wake up. Someone called Maggie is here for you."

Panic shot through her. *Maggie?* What could her sister possibly be doing at *Aphrodite?* Throwing off the covers, Agatha scrambled to dress, her fingers trembling as she hastily pulled on her gown. Without waiting to arrange her hair properly, she rushed to the door, yanking it open to find Bea waiting with a concerned expression.

"Where is she?" Agatha demanded, her voice barely steady.

"In the small parlor downstairs." Bea hesitated, her brow furrowing. She's pacing and seems very upset."

Agatha was already flying down the stairs, her heart thudding painfully. Her mind raced with a hundred scenarios, each more dreadful than the last. When she reached the parlor, she found Maggie pacing, wringing her hands together, her face streaked with tears. Agatha's heart clenched at the sight of her younger sister's palpable distress.

"Maggie!" Agatha rushed toward her. "What is wrong?"

Maggie turned, and without warning, she burst into tears, her shoulders shaking violently.

"It's Carson," she sobbed, her voice choked. "He's taken ill again ... He's abed with a fever, and Gloria is beside herself with worry. We—"

Her breath hitched as more tears spilled down her cheeks. "We asked the local physician to come, but we didn't have the full amount of coins required to pay him, so he refused. He didn't even see him, Agatha. He didn't come."

Agatha felt the world tilt around her. Carson was ill again and without proper care. Her breath quickened, fear clawing at her chest. It had taken her brother several weeks to recover from the last bout of illness.

"We ... what if ..." Maggie's words broke into a sob, and she collapsed into Agatha's arms. "What if by the time we return, Carson is ..."

"No," Agatha cut her off, her voice fierce despite the fright racing through her. "No, don't think like that. He will be alright. Carson only needs a good physician."

But her words felt hollow, even to herself. She closed her eyes and breathed deeply, pushing the feelings down. Without a clear mind, she would not serve her family well. Agatha broke away from her sister and hurried toward Madam Rebecca's door. She needed money immediately. But as she neared the door, a burly footman stepped in her path, his arm outstretched to block her way.

"The Madam is meeting with Mr. Wright," he said, his voice low and firm. "They are not to be disturbed."

Agatha froze, the name chilling her. Mr. Wright. The ruthless gambling den owner her father had owed. "This is *urgent*. I must speak with Madam Rebecca right away."

"Mr. Wright is not a man that can be disobeyed," he said. "I cannot allow anyone to enter and disturb their meeting. Unless *Aphrodite* is on fire."

"When will the meeting end?"

"They must not be disturbed before seven."

"That is hours away," Agatha gasped.

Her mind spun, and everything around her seemed to close in for a moment. She couldn't wait. Maggie's cries pierced her, and Agatha's heart twisted painfully. If they were delayed any longer, what would happen to her brother? "Come with me, Maggie."

She rushed from *Aphrodite* with her sister on her heels, hailing the first hackney carriage she saw on the street. Her hands shook as she climbed inside, shuffling over on the seat so her sister could sit beside her.

"Where to, miss?" the driver asked, his voice gruff.

"Grosvenor Square," Agatha said, giving him the address.

It was desperate, reckless even, but she had no other choice. Thomas was the only person she knew with enough power and means to help Carson. The carriage lurched forward, and Agatha leaned back, her mind racing. Agatha's mind raced with uncertainty, bracing herself for what she might say to Thomas. She only hoped he was home. Beside her, Maggie's quiet sobs tugged at her heart, but Agatha could find no words of comfort. She kept her eyes closed for a moment, forcing herself to control the rising panic. When the hackney finally arrived at his townhouse, she quickly paid the driver a shilling, asking him to wait for his full fare.

As Agatha reached the door, she rapped the knocker sharply. It swung open, revealing a dignified gentleman who peered down at her with evident disdain.

"Inform Lord Radbourne that Miss Woodville is here to call. It is urgent."

"Lord Radbourne is not receiving visitors today, madam. Please present your card—"

Agatha swept past him, heedless of propriety. Her heart hammered as she searched for any sign of Thomas in the grand entrance hall.

"Agatha?"

The sound of his steady and commanding voice almost made her knees buckle. Thomas moved down the hall toward her, his gaze sweeping her with concern.

"Are you hurt?"

Her throat tightened. "I ..." She drew a shuddering breath, willing her voice not to break. "I need help. Will you help me?"

"Yes." His answer was immediate, resolute.

She took another breath, steadying herself, a tremor of relief rushing through her heart. "You don't even know what I need—"

"It doesn't matter. Tell me."

"My brother is gravely ill. My stepmother tried to call on the village physician, but he refused to come without a fee. I ..." She swallowed, casting a glance at the hackney waiting at the drive. "I need to borrow money for the carriage and the doctor. I promise to repay you with interest."

An inscrutable look entered his eyes, a

flicker of something that sent warmth rushing through her chest.

"Do not insult me by speaking of repayment."

His gaze shifted to Maggie, who was peeking up at him with wide, teary eyes.

"Is this your sister?"

Agatha nodded. "This is Maggie. Maggie, this is the Earl of Radbourne."

Maggie attempted a curtsy but abandoned it, her awe-stricken gaze fixed on Thomas.

He smiled gently. "Pleased to meet you, Maggie." He turned and motioned them to follow. "Come with me."

They trailed him down the long corridor. Agatha felt a surge of gratitude and relief as Thomas instructed his butler.

"Prepare my carriage with the fastest horses and summon Dr. Preston without delay. He is to attend Miss Woodville's family with all haste and pay the waiting fare."

Less than an hour later, they were on their way to Devonshire in a grand carriage drawn by four powerful horses. Agatha and Maggie sat inside with the physician while Thomas rode ahead on a magnificent black stallion, cutting a striking figure. Agatha, exhausted and emotionally drained, leaned back against the plush squabs, a faint thrill of wonder at how much she trusted Thomas to manage everything. She had long relied on her own self-sufficiency, and it unnerved her to realize how quickly she allowed him a space no one had ever occupied. Yet, despite her best efforts, she couldn't summon the energy to build her usual defenses. She let her eyes drift closed, surrendering to the rhythmic sway of the carriage and the rare comfort of not bearing the weight alone.

CHAPTER 22

Agatha perched on a wooden stool, a smile
gracing her lips as she watched Thomas
inhale the rich aroma of freshly baked bread. Six
loaves lay before them, their golden crusts warm
and inviting, each brushed with melted butter
that made her mouth water. She felt a rush of
pride; she had made these herself, wanting to
thank him in her own way for everything he had
done.

The four-day journey from London to her
home in Devonshire had been an adventure and
an agony of its own, each moment drawing her
closer to Thomas. They'd shared days on the
road, stopping only briefly at inns to catch a few
hours of sleep. Each night, Thomas and Dr.
Preston took a separate room while Agatha
shared with Maggie. Yet, as darkness fell and the
inn grew quiet, she would find herself slipping

from her bed. Every night, she found Thomas leaning against the door in the hallway, waiting. His gaze, warm and mysterious, would deepen as she approached.

They stayed in the hallway, sometimes talking and sometimes in silence until exhaustion claimed her. In those quiet hours, she would lean against his shoulder, her defenses nonexistent, and let herself bask in his strength and presence. Agatha had never felt more protected nor more vulnerable to him.

At last, they arrived in Devonshire. Carson was still gravely ill, his fever raging, but Dr. Preston immediately took charge, bringing a measure of calm and reassurance to everyone. It took two days of round-the-clock care, worry etched in every brow, but her brother's fever finally broke. Relief flooded through her, and now, that very morning, Carson had joined Maggie and Sarah outside, his laughter echoing as he played with a kite.

And here was Thomas, looking at her with that same warmth as he reached for a warm slice of bread, the butter melting into it. He took a bite, savoring the taste, and closed his eyes.

"This," he said, "might be the best thing I've tasted in years."

Liar, she tenderly whispered, imagining how lavish his menu must be as an earl.

Still, warmth spread through her chest. "Try this one next; it has raisins and honey."

"Delicious," he replied, taking a bite.

She grinned, the lightness she felt impossible to contain. "Thomas, I will repay the monies you advance to buy food and—"

"I will take pleasure in turning you over my knees and pinkening your arse if you speak about repayment. You don't owe me anything." His tone was gentle but firm.

Her fierce pride stirred inside her chest. "Friends allow friends to repay generosity."

"Is it important to you to repay me?"

She swallowed. "Yes."

He leaned in, his gaze steady and affectionate. "Very well. Repay me with loaves of bread whenever I want."

"Thomas?"

"Hmm?"

"Do you think we will remain friends after the auction? How likely will we ever cross each other's paths again?"

He faltered into remarkable stillness, his expression turning almost cold and indifferent.

"Do not answer it," she said, her chest tightening.

He nodded once, reaching for another slice of bread. His gaze on her face felt too piercing, yet she could not read what he thought.

Agatha felt excessively silly for asking the question, even as the ache inside her chest deepened.

They sat in comfortable silence, children's laughter drifting through the window. Agatha's heart twisted with gratitude and that thumping ache.

"Agatha," he murmured, his gaze softening, "If you do not object, I will visit you again here."

The words settled over her like a warm blanket. The idea was laughable: a man of consequence like Thomas returning to this modest cottage to call upon one like her. It stung, though, knowing that his life would always remain worlds apart from hers. Even now, he and the physician stayed at the village inn, their small home too cramped to accommodate such esteemed guests.

"Everyone will be in an uproar over the delay in the auction," he said, his tone even, controlled. "To capitalize on it, we should start our return journey to London today. I'll arrange for Dr. Preston to stay another week to ensure little Carson fully recovers."

Agatha reached across the table, her fingers grazing his hand. To her surprise, he didn't pull away. "Thank you," she whispered.

Thomas lowered his gaze to their joined hands, a look of contemplation crossing his face before he lifted his eyes to hers. His expression held an intensity that made her pulse race.

"Would you consider being my mistress?"

The question landed like a blow, so unexpected and shocking that she jerked her hand back, her heart pounding furiously.

"What ... what would that mean?" she stammered, a painful warmth filling her cheeks.

"It would mean," he said steadily, his gaze unwavering, "that you wouldn't need to auction yourself. I would provide a comfortable home, with servants to tend to you and an allowance for your needs. I'd take you to London, Paris, Venice ... wherever you want. And," he added, his voice softening with the slightest hint of hunger, "I would take you to my bed whenever we both wanted. I'd try not to get you with child."

A maelstrom of emotions crashed over Agatha, an unfamiliar ache tightening her chest as she struggled to control her expression. She hadn't realized how foolishly she'd hoped for something more, even as she knew better. It was foolish, she knew, to feel hurt. A man of his stature could never offer her anything beyond a fleeting arrangement. Blinking against the sting of tears, she forced herself to meet his gaze.

"I gather there's still a chance one might fall pregnant even if attempts are made to prevent it," she said, her voice steady though her heart felt anything but.

"Yes," he replied, his tone equally controlled.

"So, if I bore your child ... they would be a bastard."

His expression grew more remote. "I would see to your care and the child's. You'd want for nothing."

The weight of his offer, so practical and devoid of genuine commitment, settled heavily on her. She withdrew her hands, lifting her chin as she met his eyes. "I could never accept such a position," she said quietly.

A flicker of disappointment crossed his face before he masked it with a jaded smile. "I thought as much," he murmured. "Very well. I'll draw up a bank draft—"

"No," she interrupted, her voice firmer than she felt. "You don't owe me anything. And I won't accept your charity, as I could never repay it."

They sat in silence, and though the intimacy of the moment shattered, she held his gaze. Though he would never be hers, she would hold fast to her dignity and the choices she made, guiding her life on her own terms.

"Very well," he said.

She rose gracefully. "I'll spend a bit of time

with Carson and Sarah. I'll be ready to depart for London within the hour."

Without waiting for a response, Agatha turned and walked away, her heart aching with every step. She was keenly aware of his gaze lingering on her as she left. The longing that pulsed inside her felt almost unbearable, yet she forced herself to keep moving, holding her head high even as her heart ached.

❦

THOMAS CALMLY CLIMBED the stairs to the fourth floor of *Aphrodite*. They had barely returned that morning. Madam Rebecca had been a whirl of anxious energy; pacing and muttering that the delay might disrupt all their plans. Still, her face lit up when she saw the turnout downstairs—a crowd of gentlemen with more wealth than they could spend in a lifetime and intrigue in their eyes.

He had told himself he would not attend, but instead of descending his carriage at White's, he was here. Agatha had requested to see him in her private room. Thomas opened the door and stepped inside, immediately struck by the delicate outline of her silhouette behind the screen. She moved with a soft grace, her shape blurred yet alluring against the dim light.

"You wanted to see me, Agatha."

"Thomas," her voice was quiet, a note of uncertainty tinged with excitement. "I ... I've been readying myself for a few hours now."

He could see the outline of her hand smoothing over her body and hear the small intake of breath before she continued: "I bathed in rose-scented water ... Bea helped me, and she massaged me with lavender oil."

Thomas stood motionless, his throat tightening. He could almost smell the lingering hint of roses and lavender in the air, and the combination seemed to weave a spell around him. Her nervousness was palpable, almost tangible, and he remained silent, letting her speak, sensing her vulnerability like an ache in his own chest.

He almost offered her money again, then recalled the fierce pride and will that had peeked from her gaze in that small cottage.

"Why did you ask to see me?"

The screen shifted as she stepped around it, revealing herself in a simple cotton robe that dwarfed her slight frame. Her hair was loosely gathered, framing her face in gentle tendrils. She looked so lovely, so unguarded, that it stole his breath.

Her eyes met his, wide and filled with a longing that she seemed to barely contain.

Agatha reached out, her hand trembling slightly, as she offered him a small silk sachet. A delicate fragrance filled the air as he took it from her. His fingers brushed hers, and he felt a jolt of warmth—something beyond mere attraction—a raw, inexplicable tenderness.

"What is this?"

She smiled, her cheeks tinging with color. "I ... I made this for you. As a thank you—for everything. Your help, your friendship. It is a perfumed sachet. I picked a fragrance ... that reminded me of you. I embroidered your initials on it."

Thomas swallowed, struggling to find words, but they stuck in his throat. The overwhelming surge of emotions almost made him want to laugh, tease her, drag her into his arms, and kiss her. Yet he couldn't be anything but silent, feeling the sachet warm in his hand, its scent faintly mingling with her own.

"Thank you."

She smiled; it was radiant and enchanting.

He slipped the sachet into his pocket, feeling its weight settle there, far heavier than its size suggested.

The silence stretched between them, and he could not break his gaze from hers, his resolve weakening with each beat of his heart.

Bloody hell.

"Are you ready?" Thomas asked, his hand folded behind his back as he carefully composed his expression into an indifferent mask.

Agatha lowered her gaze briefly, and he detected the faint tremor as it worked through her slender frame. "Yes."

His gut twisted, that unfamiliar emotion pressing against the barrier he'd long perfected. "I will not be staying."

Her head snapped up, her eyes almost wide and pleading, and Thomas felt something tighten further, painfully. He did not want to watch the man who would win her take her away. "Agatha—"

"Stay, please," she whispered, her voice so soft it was barely audible. "If only for the first few minutes. I'm certain I'll bumble the moment I step out there. If you were there ... if I could look up to the balcony and see you ... I wouldn't be so anxious."

He couldn't refuse her. "I'll stay, but only for a few minutes," he said, the words taut, a promise he didn't wish to make but found himself compelled to.

She smiled. "Thomas?"

"Yes."

"Will ... will I ever see you again? I know I asked before, but I wish only for your honest answer."

He hesitated. "I'm leaving town for Bath. When I return, you'll likely no longer be here."

The words felt almost brittle, and though he kept his tone curt, something pained lingered in his chest.

"I see," she murmured. "Thomas ... I will ... miss you."

Damn it all to hell. Her words burned into him. *I will miss you, too, Agatha.* Yet he didn't say it aloud. Instead, he dipped his head, cupping her face gently as he pressed his lips to hers in a brief kiss.

"Farewell, Agatha. I hope you find success this evening."

"Thank you, Thomas, and thank you for all your lessons. Tonight would not have been possible without your help."

He turned abruptly, leaving her chamber.

"Oh, God," she whispered just as he shut the door behind him, her voice a soft echo in his mind.

Thomas forced himself down the stairs, his footsteps echoing louder than his own racing pulse.

What the hell was wrong with him? He pressed his hand to his chest, startled by the ache that had taken root there. He wanted to turn back, to tell her how she lingered in his thoughts, her laughter and quick wit like a lure.

Agatha Woodville was a woman he was certain would haunt him—not just in the coming weeks, but perhaps for years.

Perhaps, he thought with dark resolve, if he had her, truly had her, even for one night, he could put her from his mind. Perhaps if he made love to her in every wicked way he'd imagined, she would no longer hold this grip on him.

Yet he couldn't bring himself to move back up those stairs.

Snarling under his breath, he forced the thought away and made his way to the first floor. The grand gambling room had been transformed, the usual smoke-filled air now charged with an air of mystery and anticipation. Heavy drapes cloaked the room in shadow, lit only by candelabras casting an amber glow. He took his place on the upper balcony, out of sight but able to see her clearly.

Only a few minutes, and then he would leave.

CHAPTER 23

Agatha's fingernails dug painfully into her palms. She released her fists and wrapped her arms around herself, hugging tightly. The fissure in her heart seemed to split even wider. The composure she had desperately tried to maintain splintered. He was leaving, and it appeared he couldn't care less that she would soon auction her virginity, her sensuality, to another. She loathed that, deep down, she wasn't sure she could go through with it.

My family needs me, she silently reminded herself, but another voice whispered, *perhaps you could accept his money and repay him in time.*

She scoffed at her own foolishness, squared her shoulders, and shed her robe. Agatha stepped into the silken skirt that sat low on her waist, and the sheer fabric covering her breasts only teased at modesty. Her belly lay bare, her décolletage framed to allure. Bea entered and began to brush her hair, accentuating her eyes with kohl.

"Are you sure about the wig?" Bea asked, watching her closely.

"Yes."

A dark red wig was affixed to her head, its dramatic tresses falling to her waist, lending her a strikingly mysterious allure. Agatha stared at herself in the mirror, seeing a provocative stranger with gleaming, confident eyes. She looked both powerful and untouchable.

Agatha took a deep breath and left her chamber, descending the winding staircase. The pleasure house had fallen silent, all anticipation toward the shadowed dais. She entered, feeling painfully exposed but empowered, her beauty a tool she had to wield expertly.

Before she looked up, she felt his gaze. She met Thomas's eyes across the room—cool, indifferent, and then they were filled with a hunger that made her pulse race. Her skin heated under the intensity of his stare. Their eyes held for several beats, and then he gave a slight nod. Agatha turned back to the crowd, knowing she now owned their curiosity.

Madam Rebecca clapped, signaling the servants to light the candles and wall sconces around the dais. Each one flared up in choreographed unison, casting a glow that highlighted the drama of the moment. A haunting flute began to play, joined by the melodic strains of a violin, both hidden behind curtains, filling the room with a captivating, seductive sound.

Agatha took a step into the light, emerging fully from the shadows.

"By God," a gentleman whispered from his seat, half-rising as if drawn to her by a force beyond his control.

"Gentlemen," Madam Rebecca's voice rang out, commanding their attention. "Allow me to present Lady W. Tonight, she will dance for you the *Raqs Sharqi*—a most sensual dance that celebrates the waist, hips, and belly, meant to tantalize and delight." She paused, her voice dripping with promise. "Lady W is a virgin."

A murmur rippled through the room, intensified by the allure of her mystery.

Madam Rebecca raised her hands, smiling as though conducting an orchestra of anticipation. "But not just any virgin. She knows how to tempt, tease, and fulfill."

Agatha nearly smirked at the exaggeration.

"You have the chance to bid for her," Madam Rebecca continued, "and if you win, five decadent nights in her arms await you. There are, however, a few limitations: no bondage, no whipping, flogging, or spanking. She will allow forced pleasure. And," Madam's voice softened, a sly smile curving her lips, "her virgin arse is also available as long as mutual pleasure is assured ... in its fucking."

Agatha's face burned at the deliberate crudeness, but she held her head high as Madam Rebecca looked at her approvingly.

"She blushes still, gentlemen," Madam Rebecca noted with a knowing grin. "Isn't that delightful? Lady W is yours to debauch. The bidding will begin after her dance."

The room fell silent, the anticipation thickening as Agatha took her first step. As the flute sprang to life, the haunting melody wound around her like an unseen lover's hands, coaxing her forward and guiding her movements. She let the music settle into her bones, each note a shivering pulse in her blood. She swayed forward, her hips rolling to the steady rhythm, feeling the collective gaze of the audience, but her awareness centered solely on Thomas.

Murmurs of appreciation rippled through the crowd, yet Agatha barely heard them. Her focus narrowed, sharpening to a single point. She was dancing for him alone. Lifting her arms gracefully above her head, Agatha arched her neck, feeling the weight of his gaze—hot and dark, brimming with an intensity she could almost touch. She met his eyes, holding them deliberately, a smile curving her lips as her hips swayed in a slow, sensual gyration meant to tempt. Heat rushed over her skin, and she knew the lavender-scented oil shimmering along her bare arms and midriff heightened her allure, catching the light like a thousand tiny stars.

It was as if the music poured into her veins, igniting a decadent fire that spread with each turn and arch of her body. Her hands traced down her sides, her fingers grazing her waist and hips, each movement a careful blend of elegance and enticement. She was aware of the way her skirt slit skimmed her thighs, teasing glimpses of her flesh with each roll and twist.

Her gaze flicked back to Thomas, and her heartbeat quickened. His heated stare sent a thrill down her spine. Agatha's every step, sway, and glide was a silent challenge to him.

Look at me. Want me. Suffer for it.

A slight sheen of sweat slicked her skin, and she welcomed the heat. The feel of it made her more acutely aware of her own body. She felt powerful, beautiful, and daring. When the music slowed, Agatha lowered her arms, her movements languid, her body curving in time with the final, lingering notes. She held Thomas's gaze until the very end before finally turning to the crowd, catching her breath. In the charged silence that followed, her body thrummed with exhilaration, her heart still racing.

"Gentlemen," Madam Rebecca called, her voice filled with practiced charm. "For five nights of bliss with Lady W, the bidding starts at one thousand pounds."

Agatha's heart leaped as a hand shot up almost immediately. "One thousand pounds."

"Eleven hundred," came another voice from somewhere in the back.

"Fifteen hundred!" someone else called.

Her pulse quickened as each voice echoed with a higher bid, a strange, taut anxiety twisting inside her. She raised her eyes to the balcony. Thomas's gaze was unreadable, and with a small dip of his head, he stepped back from the railing, turning away from the bidding. He wouldn't stay.

Her chest tightened painfully, and she bit the inside of her lip, the sharp sting grounding her. She blinked back the tears that threatened, heat prickling at the edges of her vision.

"Six thousand pounds!" a gentleman's voice rang out, and the tremor running through her body was unmistakable.

Delight sparkled in Madam Rebecca's eyes, but Agatha felt a mounting dread.

Don't be silly, she told herself, pushing down the panic that coiled within her.

To her shock, the bidding continued with no sign of slowing.

"We're at eight thousand pounds," Madam Rebecca announced with a pleased smile. "Do we have another bid?"

"It seems Lord Humphrey will—"

"Eight thousand five hundred," came Lord Humphrey's steady reply.

"Nine thousand!" another voice called.

The room stilled, each breath held in suspense.

"Nine thousand two hundred," Lord Humphrey raised, his voice edged with determination.

Lord Benedict surged to his feet, his eyes flashing. "Nine thousand five hundred."

The air grew thick with anticipation as the bidding had narrowed to these two rivals.

"Ten thousand pounds!" Madam Rebecca's voice rose, elation clear in her tone. "Do we have another bid?"

Agatha's belly clenched, her fingers digging into her palms as she fought to remain poised.

Madam Rebecca waited a few beats and then said, "Lord Benedict—"

"Eleven thousand pounds," a new voice cut through the din.

Her breath caught. *Thomas!* A jolt of relief and fierce, unsteady emotion seized her heart. She scanned the crowd, desperate for a glimpse of him.

Lord Benedict scowled, glancing back as if assessing his rival.

"Eleven thousand one hundred," he spat, his tone laced with frustration.

"Twelve thousand," came Thomas's reply, his tone bored and indifferent.

The room went still as her heart hammered wildly. *Where is he?*

"Twelve thousand three hundred—"

"Fifteen thousand pounds."

The entire room fell silent as Thomas's voice rang out, cool and commanding.

A murmur of astonishment swept through the crowd. Lord Benedict's face flushed with frustration, and he opened his mouth as if to retort but then stopped, slumping back in his chair, defeated. Madam Rebecca looked positively delighted, her eyes wide as she leaned forward, clasping her hands in triumph.

"Gentlemen," she announced, barely containing her exhilaration. "The winning bid of fifteen thousand pounds goes to Lord Radbourne!"

Scattered conversation filled the room. Agatha's heart raced, her pulse pounding with excitement and disbelief. Thomas emerged from the shadows, his gaze intense as he approached the dais. Without a word, he stepped onto the stage, reaching for her. The crowd's murmurs faded, blending into a distant hum as he slipped his arms around her and lifted her effortlessly, cradling her against his chest. She wrapped her arms around his neck, her face inches from his, and his scent enveloped her, intoxicating her senses. She barely noticed the stunned gazes and whispers as he carried her from the room, her whole being focused solely on him.

They ascended the stairs, the familiar hallways of *Aphrodite* falling away as he carried her to the fourth floor, his private quarters. Agatha's gaze never left his face, her breath coming in shallow gasps. She couldn't speak or bring herself to break the charged silence between them. Every sensation was heightened, each step bringing her closer to being in his arms. Her awareness of him, his strength, the gentle but possessive hold he kept around her, was so intense it was almost painful.

"Will you ... stay for five nights?" she finally asked, unable to bear not knowing how long he would stay with her.

Thomas's gaze flickered, a shadow of something unreadable crossing his eyes. "One," he replied, his voice a low, steady murmur. Her heart twisted, and she barely had time to process his words before he stopped at the door, pushed it open, and carried her into his private chamber.

"Only tonight."

CHAPTER 24

Thomas's mouth crashed against Agatha's, and she was instantly drenched with desire. His lips were firm and demanding, and she melted into him, her body responding with an urgency that left her breathless. He stroked his tongue against hers, drawing her deeper into the kiss, igniting a fire that spread through her veins. He slanted his head to deepen the kiss, and she curled her tongue around his, savoring his taste, his heat. With desperate haste, she started pulling at his cravat with the one hand she didn't have locked around the back of his neck to keep his mouth where it belonged.

Still kissing, he stumbled with her to the wall, breaking their kiss to spin her to face the wall. Agatha moaned, arching her neck when he buried his mouth there, sucking at the flesh covering her madly hammering pulse. His hands dragged up the thin, silken skirt, and two fingers plunged into her already wet sex.

He grunted, and then he arched her hip with one hand, and with the other, he positioned his cock at her sex and pressed inward. Whimpering at the unyielding pressure, she flexed her hips. Her lover moved his hips in a short, powerful thrust that seated him halfway into her.

"Thomas!" Pain and pleasure spread from where they joined.

"You are so hot and tight," he murmured against her ear, his voice rough with desire.

He thrust his fingers through her hair, arching her neck even more. The kiss pressed along her throat was tender, yet his other hand trailed over her quivering belly with domineering carnality. Thomas's hands went lower, delving through her curls to find her clitoris.

"I am too desperate for you to go slow," he growled, his voice a low rumble that vibrated through her.

Agatha whimpered, finding it difficult to focus on anything but the stretching tightness between her thighs. He dragged three of his fingers over her aching nub, piercing the sensitive flesh with pleasure, and the honeyed heat blossomed through her.

"I do not want slow," she gasped, her voice trembling with need.

Another drag over her clitoris made her cry out. The sweet rush of ecstasy made Agatha sharply arch her hips, her buttocks nestling more into his body, driving the impalement of his cock even deeper.

"Do you know what I like?" he asked, his voice a dark promise.

"Yes," she whispered, her breath hitching. It had been revealed in every lesson, every shared laughter, and every wicked kiss.

"I am going to fuck your pussy, your mouth, and your arse for the night. It is going to hurt sometimes, but I promise I will make it so damn good for you."

Agatha dropped her head weakly onto his shoulder, her arousal so strong sharp tremors wracked her body. "Yes," she breathed, her voice barely a whisper.

Thomas lifted her against him, his hands strong and sure as he carried her to the bed. He laid her gently on her stomach, then slid his left arm under her belly and drew her onto her knees, raising her hips and positioning her for him with strong hands. He spread her thighs wide, fisted his cock, and rubbed it over her folds.

"Thomas, you have been teasing me for days! I want—"

Her cry choked off when he hammered his cock to the hilt. She collapsed onto her elbows, her derriere provocatively arched as he balanced her on the edge of pain and ecstasy. Thomas withdrew his cock, her sex clinging so tightly to his girth, she felt every inch of him as he retreated and then sank back inside her to the hilt again. He slowly pumped his hips over and over, his strokes lazy until sensations gathered and coiled tight in her belly. Thomas's thrusts grew more urgent, each one driving deeper into her.

"Play with your clitoris," he groaned.

Agatha moaned, her fingers whispering over her belly to find her nub. She shuddered, feeling very sensitive there, yet that heightened the pleasure. She strummed her clitoris, whimpering as the heat bloomed hotter. Thomas gripped her hips tightly, his fingers digging into her flesh as he worked his cock harder and deeper into her sex. Agatha's body trembled under his carnal assault, her breath coming in ragged gasps. The sensations were overwhelming, a mix of erotic pain and pleasure that twisted together in a knot of raw desire.

"Thomas, please ..." she whimpered, her voice breaking as she struggled to find words.

"Shh, just feel," he murmured, his voice a low, hungry sound.

His thrusts became more rhythmic; each one timed perfectly to send waves of pleasure crashing through her. Her fingers found her clitoris again, rubbing in slow, deliberate circles that sent sparks of sensation shooting through her. Sensations gathered within, and each stroke pushed her closer to the edge of bliss.

Thomas's hips snapped harder as if he could sense her impending release.

"Oh!" she cried as she finally shattered.

Agatha convulsed, her inner walls clenching around his cock as wave after wave of pleasure washed over her. She moaned his name, her body shuddering with the force of her release. Thomas slowed his pace, his thrusts becoming more gentle, more tender, as he held her close, his breath hot against her ear.

"You're amazing," he whispered.

His voice was hoarse with arousal and tension. Agatha could only nod, her body still trembling from the intensity of her orgasm. She felt drained yet still so full of desire. Thomas pulled out of her, his cock glistening. He turned her onto her back, his eyes dark with lust as he looked down at her. He pressed his thumb against her clitoris and started to rub. Thomas smiled, a wicked, knowing smile, as he lowered his head between her legs. He buried his face into her pussy, his tongue stroking her sensitive flesh with a greed that left her breathless. He teased her clitoris with his tongue, sending sharp jolts of pleasure shooting through her. His fingers found her entrance, slipping inside her as his tongue continued its relentless assault.

Agatha's body tensed again, her breath coming in short, sharp gasps. The sensations were overwhelming, her sex aching, yet pleasure still drowned her thoughts. Thomas's tongue and fingers worked in perfect harmony, driving her closer and closer to the edge.

"Thomas, please ... I can't ..." she gasped, her voice breaking as she struggled to find words.

"Shh, just let go," he murmured, his voice muffled against her flesh.

His fingers thrust into her with increasing urgency, his tongue flicking over her clitoris with relentless precision. Another swell of ecstasy crashed over her senses, and she twisted, trying to escape his mouth. Strong hands clasped her hips and held her under the lash of his mouth.

"*Thomas!*" she cried, thrusting her fingers through his hair.

His answering groan of pleasure reverberated through her entire body. Agatha trembled; the pleasure was too intense. Thomas rose above her, nudging her thighs wide to settle between her legs. Her heartbeat throbbed against her ears as he explored the lines of her hips, belly, and breasts. Every touch ignited a deeper flash of pleasure. He started a slow, deliberate massage of her breasts, fingers tugging and rolling her nipples.

His thumb came to rest against her softly parted lips. Thomas kissed right at the hollow of her throat, over her fiercely beating pulse, down to her nipple and sucked it into his mouth.

"That feels so good," she said, moaning.

He released her and kissed her mouth, his eyes open and peering into hers. Agatha's heart trembled at the lust and the tenderness in his eyes. She had the alarming thought that he could sense that he made her heart ache for impossible things with him. Thomas slid his cock inside her sex. Despite her overflowing wetness, she gasped at the almost painful stretch. She slipped her legs high around his back, arching into him. This close, she could see the beauty, lust, and tenderness in his gaze. His thick cock dragged in and out, pleasure jarring her with each thrust. Agatha never imagined coupling could be so consuming. He wrenched her cries and moans and climaxes, each one more intense than the last. Her fingers raked his sweat-slicked skin, her pussy starting to ache and her thighs trembling, yet her lover gave her little rest.

His mouth took hers, his tongue gliding against hers, a perfect mimicry of his plunging cock. Her body tensed, drawn tight as the pleasure built. The swell that slammed into her belly felt as if it broke Agatha apart, cascading heat through her. This climax was more intense than the previous three—or was it four? She couldn't keep count, lost in the whirlwind of sensation.

Thomas groaned, pulling from her body to release his seed on her quivering belly. He leaned down, his lips brushing against her ear. "Our night has just started."

Her breath hitched at his words, a shiver running down her spine. She could still feel the remnants of her climax, her body trembling with the aftershocks. Thomas's hands roamed her body, his touch possessive, almost reverent.

"You're so beautiful," he murmured. "So perfectly responsive. I could spend hours inside you, feeling your cunt clench around me, hearing you scream my name."

She could feel her arousal building again, her pussy throbbing with need. Thomas's hands moved lower, his fingers tracing the curve of her hip before dipping between her thighs. Oh, the pleasure was exquisite.

"Your tight little pussy is still so wet," he said, his voice laced with satisfaction. "Do you want more, Agatha?"

She nodded.

"Tell me," he demanded. His cock, still hard and throbbing, pressed against her entrance. "Tell me what you want."

"I want you," she gasped, her voice trembling with desire. "I want you to make love to me over and over as you promised."

"And when your pussy is too sore?"

Their gazes held.

"Then my mouth is yours ... and when my throat cannot take more ... my arse is yours."

"*Fuck*," he hissed, dropping his forehead to hers, a sharp tremor wracking his body, his cock filling her with a force that left her breathless.

"Hold me for the night, Thomas," she whispered, her fingers curling around his nape, "and do not let me go."

His mouth brushed hers in a tender kiss, and a lump rose in her throat. Agatha swallowed down the words of love stirring in her chest, choosing instead to surrender fully to the passion blazing wickedly between them.

THOMAS STOOD BY THE BED, gazing at Agatha's serene, sleeping face. Her lashes cast delicate shadows across her cheeks, and her lips parted in a soft sigh. The hint of a smile lingered there, and he knew it was exhausted and satisfied. She looked so beautiful and utterly at peace.

A wry smile tugged at his mouth. He moved carefully, easing out of bed without making a sound. The early dawn light filtered through the curtains, casting the room in a gentle, silvery glow. He dressed quietly, knowing this encounter was likely a final farewell. Before Thomas left, he leaned down, pressing a gentle kiss to her forehead. She murmured his name, her lips curving faintly as if, even in sleep, she dreamed about it. For a moment, he nearly stopped, nearly let himself settle back into that bed and pull her into his arms. But instead, he let her drift, untouched by the weight of what lingered unsaid between them. Standing by the door, he took one last look at her, committing every detail to memory. And then, with a deep breath, he turned and walked away.

Once outside, he inhaled the cool night air, tipping his head back and breathing deeply. The sadness in her gaze, which she quickly hid before curling up beside him and drifting to sleep, haunted him. He'd taken her four times throughout the night, remembering her softly whispered plea for a break. But he hadn't paused —one night was all they had, and every second, every kiss, every release was precious. Each time he drove her toward wicked, breathless pleasure, a dark part of him wanted to punish her with ecstasy, to brand her for making him feel so damn much.

The sting of unshed tears startled him, burning hot behind his eyes. What the hell was this? He blew a harsh breath, raking his fingers through his hair and walking toward his parked carriage. Less than an hour later, Thomas climbed the steps to his bedchamber in his townhouse. Dawn was barely breaking, and he heard the stirrings of the household as he went into his room. Stripping down, he sprawled onto the bed, Agatha's scent lingering on his skin and tongue. She was gone now, a lover who had left him with only a powerful memory. But now that it was over, he swore he'd excise it from his mind. She would not haunt him.

Thomas would not allow it.

PRECISELY TWELVE DAYS LATER, Thomas realized he was a damn fool. The relentless storm inside him could no longer be ignored. He thought he could avoid his feelings and sidestep whatever emotional chaos had taken root. But the quiet nights only amplified the disarray in his heart, mirroring his inner turmoil. Agatha Woodville occupied his thoughts as persistently as the rising sun, and each attempt to bury his feelings in reports or parliamentary plans only made them grow sharper and more demanding.

A humorless smile touched his mouth. After days of restless nights recounting every moment shared, he wrote her a simple note, asking how her brother was and requesting to call on her in Devonshire. Yet the response from his runner was far from reassuring: the cottage in Devonshire was empty, and discreet inquiries suggested Miss Woodville might still be in London—last seen at *Aphrodite*.

When he read the report, Thomas rose from his desk, summoning his horse. Almost an hour later, he strode into *Aphrodite*, headed straight to Rebecca's office, and threw the door open.

She looked up, startled. "Radbourne!"

"Where is she?" he demanded, his voice tense. "And why is she still here?"

Madam Rebecca arched a brow, leaning back, an odd look flickering in her eyes. She sighed. "You're a bit late, Radbourne. Agatha accepted the protection of the Duke of Merrick. She is to be his mistress."

Her words struck like a blow to his chest, so

strong he felt winded. A *mistress*? His eyes slid
shut as pain gripped him, so visceral he rubbed
his chest. Agatha, the woman he cared for,
under the protection of another man. Another
fierce, clawing ache tore through his chest, so
raw and visceral it nearly dragged a snarl from
his throat. The thought churned, but something
in him refused to believe it. His eyes snapped
open, and his gaze bore into Rebecca.

"You lie to me?"

She stiffened, taken aback. "Radbourne—"

"Agatha would *never* agree to be any man's
mistress, not even if the king himself begged
her. Do you think because she auctioned her
virginity, you understand her character? Agatha
has more strength, honor, and pride than you or
I could ever grasp. Don't insult her again.
Whatever relationship we had will be over."

Rebecca flinched, then, after a moment,
lowered her gaze and exhaled. "I apologize," she
said softly. "I didn't think it through or expect
you would burst in here like this. My instinctive
thought was to spare her further pain. Her eyes
... when she left she had been crying, and I could
tell that she had foolishly fallen under your
charm. What is the point of you chasing her? I
know you can persuade her with seductions, but
she deserves ..."

Madam Rebecca glanced away.

"Then tell me where she went," he said.

Rebecca studied him as if weighing the sincerity of his anger. "Are you certain she's no longer here or with the duke?"

"Yes. The woman I fell in love with, the woman I am certain holds a similar regard, would not so easily betray her feelings. She's shown me her kindness, resilience, loyalty, and passion ... she's shown me herself, her pride and her determination. I broke her heart when I left without a conversation or a proper farewell. I disappointed her by hiding my feelings instead of opening myself to her. Still, she would not run from my arms to another."

Rebecca shook her head in faint disbelief. "All of my most distinguished clients have succumbed to this cursed lovesickness. First, the Duke of Basil, then the Marquess of Ambrose, Mr. Armstrong, and now you."

Thomas's brow furrowed. "Brandon?"

Rebecca chuckled. "He came only yesterday and asked Bea to marry him. The poor chit turned him down and ran off in tears. He's on a ship to Boston now, presumably heartbroken. I didn't care for her moping, so I gave her my blessing to go after him. She sailed this morning." A small, bittersweet smile crossed Rebecca's face.

"Where is Agatha? My man said she was here

a few days ago."

Rebecca sighed, her eyes softening. "I don't know. She left mere hours after you did that morning. She only returned to give me an envelope to hand you."

He frowned. "The bank draft I sent—"

"Another foolish one, Miss Woodville. After all that work, she refused to take it." Rebecca went to her desk and opened it, looking regretfully at it. "She said she could not receive payment for spending the night in your arms. She allowed me to give her five hundred pounds and left the draft here, promising to repay my loan one day."

Thomas took the draft, stuffed it into his pocket and walked away. He had already separated Madam Rebecca's cut and made a draft of seven thousand pounds to her and ten thousand pounds to Agatha. By the time he reached outside, he was smiling.

You lovely fool, Agatha.

AGATHA STOOD in the gentle morning light, a watering can in hand, sprinkling water over the rows of herbs and small flowers she had so lovingly tended these last few weeks. The salty air mingled with the scent of lavender and rosemary from her garden. It had taken time and patience, but she had carefully cultivated each plant, drawing a modest beauty from the earth before their small seaside cottage.

Her family adored the sea. She could hear their laughter faintly as they played further down the beach, relishing the freedom and the fresh air. Moving them to the coast had been a decision both reckless and right. She had only taken a loan from Madam Rebecca, who had been more than willing to lend it, having made a fortune from the night of the bidding. With cautious planning, she knew this money could last for three years, enough time, she hoped, to come up with a longer-term solution.

But today, as she watered the delicate leaves, tears pricked her eyes and slipped down her face. She felt like a fool, remembering the ten thousand pounds she had turned down. Ten thousand that could have secured their future indefinitely. *If I'd accepted it, perhaps we'd have some certainty*, but her heart twisted, protesting the notion.

A harsh sob tore from her, and she pressed a trembling hand to her mouth. She had lost far more than money, far more than security. Six weeks had passed since she'd woken alone in the bed at *Aphrodite*, the space beside her cold and empty, and the ache in her chest had not lessened. She missed Thomas fiercely and hated herself for falling in love with a man she could not keep, whose station and heart were worlds apart.

Wiping her tears on the corner of her apron, Agatha took a shaky breath, trying to steady herself. Her heart still beat unsteadily with longing. She'd built a life around her family and her love for them, yet Thomas had found a place in her soul that she hadn't known existed.

"Agatha."

His voice was so unexpected and familiar that she froze, her watering can slipping from her hand. She turned, her heart slamming in her chest, and there he stood—Thomas. He looked as impossibly handsome as ever, his gaze searing and intense as it locked onto hers. She felt rooted to the spot, her breath caught in her throat, unable to believe he was real and standing before her.

"Thomas?" Her voice was a mere whisper.

His gaze swept over her, softened by something she hadn't seen before—a mixture of relief and regret.

"You are a hard woman to find."

"You ... you were searching?"

"Yes. It took my man of affairs and a few investigators almost a month. I've missed you," he said, his voice rough.

The simple yet powerful words tore down her defenses, and fresh tears filled Agatha's eyes. She took an unsteady step forward, her breath hitching, before she faltered, uncertain.

"Agatha ..." His voice was low, edged with urgency.

She fisted her hands at her sides, a quiet tremor running through her. "*Why* are you here?"

He stepped closer, his gaze steady and sincere. "I missed you, Agatha, and it took me too long to realize I don't want to go on in this life without you. I want all of you—your honesty, fears, dreams, and hopes. I don't say these words lightly."

His eyes were unwavering as they held hers. "You don't have to tell me you're fine if you're not; I don't want that. You don't have to carry every feeling and struggle alone."

Her heart thundered as he continued, his words cutting through her lingering doubts.

"You don't have to hide behind a façade or give me what you think others expect. I want to understand you completely, even the parts you'd prefer to keep to yourself. I want your laughter and your tears. I want your sweet, wicked smile. I want your kindness, your generosity. I am greedy. I promise you will never want anything in this life. I promise to give you all of me."

Her breath hitched. "May I share your pain and struggles, if you have them?"

"Yes. Always."

An indescribable feeling rose in her heart. Agatha broke. With a soft sob, she hurtled into his arms, her shoulders trembling as she clung to him. His hand moved to her back, fingers pressing into her as if he couldn't let her go.

"What is it?" he demanded, his voice rough. "Why are you crying?"

She sniffed, her voice breaking. "What took you so long?" She gripped his shirt, then, as if punishing him, pinched his arm with a trembling hand. "I *missed* you so much, Thomas. I thought I'd never see you again. I have been wretched!"

He wrapped his arms around her, holding her tightly, his face pressed into her hair. She leaned back slightly, her gaze meeting his, her red-rimmed eyes and trembling lips revealing the depth of her heartache, yet she did not care. Taking a shaky breath, she whispered, "I won't leave here. I ... will be your lover, Thomas ..., but I can't abandon my family. I want to be with you, but I need to spend time here with them and ... I don't want to bring a child into the world like that."

He dropped his hands from her waist, his gaze piercing.

"Thomas?"

He cupped her face, his thumb brushing a tear from her cheek. "Agatha," he murmured, his voice raw with emotion. "Forgive me for not saying this sooner. I *love* you. I have never loved anyone as I love you and never will. If you'll have me ... I want you as more than a lover. I want you as my friend, my wife, my countess."

Shock, joy, love, and relief flooded her heart in equal measure. "You ... you want to marry me?"

"Yes."

"I could not be a *countess*. What nonsense are you saying? Your countess?"

"Yes." Good humor gleamed in his eyes. "We will be highly unconventional and disreputable together. Do not forget what Ronald told you: I can do anything. No one would dare lift their fans to whisper about you."

She laughed, delight rushing through her. She wanted this man with a breathlessness that knew no bounds ... and she would not shy or run from the awareness of it. Agatha was willing to defy anything to be with him, even wagging tongues and gossip.

He smiled, reaching into his pocket. "I have been carrying a special license, just in case. But we could have a grand wedding at Hanover if you wish—"

"No, I don't want to wait," Agatha laughed,

wrapping her arms around his waist and pressing her face to his chest. Happiness gathered in a sweet ache in her chest. "I love you, Thomas, and I don't want to wait."

"Thank God," he said gruffly, holding her close.

As Thomas lowered his lips to hers, Agatha kissed him with all the emotion and love inside her heart.

❦

THANK you for reading *In a Rake's Embrace*! You will see peeks of Agatha and Thomas's continued love in Midnight Rendezvous (Sins & Sensibilities, Book 4). An exclusive excerpt of their wedding will be available in my publisher's newsletter this month—be sure to sign up for sneak peeks, cover reveals, and giveaways!

With love,
Stacy

❦

DEAR READERS,

From the bottom of our hearts, thank you for being part of our journey. We're Stacy and Du'Sean, the husband-and-wife duo behind our small but passionate publishing house. Our mission is to uplift diverse voices, especially those often overlooked in the romance genre, and bring their beautiful stories to life. We know how challenging it has been for authors of color to find a place in the industry, and we're committed to changing that, one book and one story at a time.

Your support means everything to us, and we'd love to stay connected! Join our **newsletter** for updates, and be sure to follow us on **Instagram**, **Facebook**, and **TikTok** for all things romance.

We adore love stories and hope you'll fall in love with the books we're honored to publish.

Reviews are also gold to authors, and we would appreciate your honest feedback on Amazon, Goodreads, and even Bookbub.

Warmest regards,

Stacy and Du'Sean

ABOUT STACY

USA Today Bestselling author Stacy Reid writes sensual Historical and Paranormal Romances and is the published author of over twenty books. Her debut novella The Duke's Shotgun Wedding was a 2015 HOLT Award of Merit recipient in the Romance Novella category, and her bestselling Wedded by Scandal series is recommended as Top picks at Night Owl Reviews, Fresh Fiction Reviews, and The Romance Reviews.

Stacy lives a lot in the worlds she creates and actively speaks to her characters (aloud). She has a warrior way "Never give up on dreams!" When she's not writing, Stacy spends a copious amount of time binge-watching series like The Walking Dead, Altered Carbon, Rise of the Phoenixes, Ten Miles of Peach Blossoms, and playing video games with her love. She also has a weakness for ice cream and will have it as her main course.

Stacy is represented by Jill Marsal at Marsal Lyon Literary Agency.

She is always happy to hear from readers and would love to connect with you via her Website,

Facebook, and Instagram. To be the first to hear about her new releases, get cover reveals, and excerpts you won't find anywhere else, sign up for her newsletter, or join her over at Historical Hellions, the fan group for her historical romance author friends, and herself!

- facebook.com/stacyreid
- instagram.com/stacy_romanceaddict
- tiktok.com/@stacy_romanceaddict
- goodreads.com/8076768.Stacy_Reid
- amazon.com/Stacy-Reid/e/B00JEVB096
- bookbub.com/authors/stacy-reid

Made in the USA
Monee, IL
08 December 2024